"You're feeling hostile toward your father,"

Jared went on in a conversational tone. "Having an affair with me would be the ultimate way of getting back at him, wouldn't it? Is that why you want to stay? To get your own brand of wild justice?"

This infuriated Cassandra. "Do you honestly think I'd have an affair with you just to . . . to—"

"To deliberately hurt your father?" Jared finished for her, still in an unperturbed voice. "I'm not sure. But I do know that you like it when I kiss you." He went on, and his voice was a fraction less cool than it had been a moment ago. "And I found it surprisingly enjoyable, as well."

Cassandra was startled. She'd been positive that Jared's sensations hadn't at all reflected hers....

JOANNA MANSELL finds writing hard work but very addictive. When she's not bashing away at her typewriter, she's usually got her nose buried in a book. She also loves gardening and daydreaming, two pastimes that go together remarkably well. The ambition of this Essex-born author is to write books that people will enjoy reading.

Books by Joanna Mansell

HARLEQUIN PRESENTS
1116—MIRACLE MAN
1139—LORD AND MASTER
1156—ILLUSION OF PARADISE
1186—THE THIRD KISS

HARLEQUIN ROMANCE
2836—THE NIGHT IS DARK
2866—SLEEPING TIGER
2894—BLACK DIAMOND

Don't miss any of our special offers. Write to us at the following address for information on our newest releases.

Harlequin Reader Service
901 Fuhrmann Blvd., P.O. Box 1397, Buffalo, NY 14240
Canadian address: P.O. Box 603,
Fort Erie, Ont. L2A 5X3

JOANNA MANSELL

wild justice

Harlequin Books

TORONTO • NEW YORK • LONDON
AMSTERDAM • PARIS • SYDNEY • HAMBURG
STOCKHOLM • ATHENS • TOKYO • MILAN

Harlequin Presents first edition November 1989
ISBN 0-373-11218-1

Original hardcover edition published in 1988
by Mills & Boon Limited

CHAPTER ONE

CASSANDRA flicked through the swatches of material, picked out the exact shade of blue that she wanted, and then tossed the others to one side. She should have felt satisfied that she had found the right colour so easily. Instead, though, she merely felt rather bored.

She tapped her fingers on the desk, impatient with herself. What the hell was wrong with her? It was just eighteen months since she had started up her interior design business. Surely she couldn't be getting tired of it already?

Perhaps the trouble was that it had all been so much easier than she had expected. Oh, she had worked hard—especially during those first few months, when she had worked all day and half the night, snatching a couple of hours' sleep whenever she could. Then satisfied clients had begun to recommend friends, and after that things had just snowballed until she had as much work as she could handle. That almost instant success had come as something of a surprise. She had known she had a good eye for colour, and an instinctive ability to recognise good style and design, instantly rejecting anything that was simply gimmicky or downright tacky. More than that, though, it turned out she had an even more important talent. After talking to a client for just a short while, she would then come up with a scheme that perfectly fitted their personality.

She always knew if they wanted frills and flounces, something stylish, or even something starkly modern.

Something, though, the fun—the challenge —seemed to have suddenly gone out of it. She was tired of picking curtains and carpets, paper and paint, furniture and fittings for people who were too busy—or too lazy!—to do it themselves. Just yesterday, surprising even herself, she had turned down a commission to oversee the redecoration of a large and prestigious country house. In fact, she had turned down several commissions during the last couple of weeks. At the moment, she had very little work lined up for the immediate future.

Perhaps she needed a holiday, she decided. She hadn't had a break since she had started up the business, so it was hardly surprising she felt tired and stale. A few days lazing around somewhere warm and sunny would probably bring back her appetite for work.

The phone suddenly rang, and she automatically reached out to pick it up. Then she stopped herself. It would almost certainly be someone offering her more work. Perhaps she should just ignore it.

Yet the phone kept ringing with a peculiarly insistent tone, until in the end she snatched it up out of pure irritation, the noise grating on her nerves.

'Yes?' she snapped, more sharply than she had intended.

'Miss Cassandra Gregory?' The voice was very definitely male, the tone cool and even.

'This is Miss Gregory,' she confirmed, for some reason being deliberately formal.

'Good. I was hoping to get hold of you in person. Do you happen to be free at the moment? If you are,

I'd like to come round and see you.'

Right now, Cassandra didn't want to see anyone. 'I'm afraid I've business appointments for the rest of the day,' she lied smoothly. 'I can't possibly fit anyone else in.'

'Surely you have a lunch hour?' the caller persisted, in that same cool tone.

'Of course I do.'

'Then perhaps you'd be willing to give up a quarter of an hour of it, in order to discuss a commission?'

Cassandra glared at the receiver. Couldn't the man take a hint? She didn't want to see him!

'I'm sorry, but it's out of the question,' she told him. 'Perhaps you could get in touch at some other time, when I'm less busy.'

Before he had a chance to reply, she quickly put down the receiver. With luck, he wouldn't ring back and that would be the last she would hear from him.

Then she gave a small grimace. If she carried on like this, it wouldn't matter if he rang back or not. Her business would have folded! It was permissible to be firm with prospective clients—some of them even liked it, especially the ones who could never make up their own minds about anything and wanted someone else to take all the decisions. Downright rudeness was definitely out, though. If she did this sort of thing too often, word would soon get around and then all those nice lucrative commissions would simply dry up.

She made herself some coffee, and then went through the swatches of blue material again. She knew perfectly well that she had picked the right shade the first time, and that she was really only killing time, but she couldn't seem to find the enthusiasm for anything else.

Glancing at her watch, she was amazed to find that it was only just gone ten o'clock. She felt as if she had already been there for hours. What was she going to do, to fill the rest of the day?

Get on with some work, she told herself sternly. But there wasn't very much to do, since she had taken on so few commissions lately. There were a few odds and ends from old jobs to be dealt with, and she still hadn't chosen the curtains for Lady Stockwell's new bedroom, but she already knew the colour she wanted. And she was *tired* of looking at material.

The outer door of her office suddenly banged, making her jump. Her part-time secretary wouldn't be in until this afternoon, which meant there was no one to deal with whoever had just come in. Cassandra sighed. She supposed she would have to see them herself. She was just getting to her feet when the door to her own office opened. The man who appeared in the doorway didn't knock. He didn't even wait to be invited in. Instead, he strode into the centre of her office and then stood there, looking down at her.

Cassandra's gaze flicked over him, absorbing a flood of first impressions. Dark hair—*very* dark. It probably looked black in some lights. And, in startling contrast, very light eyes. Green? Pale blue? she wondered. But they didn't seem to have any colour in them at all. Instead, they glittered with a quicksilver quality which she found more than a little unnerving. Rather hurriedly, her gaze slid down from his face and studied his clothes. Nothing to worry about there, she decided. He was dressed very conventionally, in a dark suit, with a light grey shirt and tie. With his oddly colourless eyes, the overall effect should have been rather dull. Yet no one was ever going to accuse this man of being any such thing, she realised with an unexpected tightening of her nerve-ends. He hadn't said a single word yet, but she already felt half flattened by his presence.

More than that, though, he gave the impression of being—well, uncivilised, she realised with a further rush of unease. It was as if the expensive clothes, the gleaming, well-cut hair, the polite expression on his face, were all a façade, a deliberately adopted disguise.

Cassandra shook her head with a sudden rush of impatience. Boredom was making her fanciful! This man was just a prospective client, that was all. And one that she wanted to get rid of as quickly as possible. She wasn't in the mood for work today.

He seemed to be studying her with equal intentness. 'Miss Cassandra Gregory?' he said at last.

With a sense of shock, she realised that she recognised that cool tone.

'You're the man who telephoned earlier,' she said at once, a hint of trepidation colouring her voice.

'Yes, I am,' he agreed. 'I believe we were—cut off.'

Was that a mocking undertone in his voice? she wondered edgily. He must know that she had put the phone down on him.

'Since we seemed to be having problems communicating with each other, I thought it would be easier if I came round in person,' he went on smoothly.

Cassandra only just managed to stop herself from scowling. In other words, he was determined to talk to her, and this was one way of making sure she couldn't refuse him!

'I'm very busy,' she said pointedly.

That quicksilver gaze slid over her near-empty desk.

'I can see that you are,' he agreed, and Cassandra glared at him. Was he mocking her again? It was impossible to tell; his expression was completely bland now. Not even a mind-reader could have worked out what was going on inside this man's head.

She sat up straight, and tried to look very businesslike as she glanced at her watch. 'Perhaps I can spare you five minutes, Mr——?'

'Sinclair,' he said, after just a moment's hesitation. 'Jared Sinclair.'

He watched her very carefully as he told her his name. Cassandra wondered why. Was she supposed to recognise it? Was the man famous, or something? Well, if he was, she certainly hadn't heard of him. The name meant nothing to her.

'Why did you want to see me, Mr Sinclair?' she asked, keeping her voice carefully polite.

Without waiting for an invitation, he slid himself into the chair on the opposite side of the desk. He should have been less intimidating now that he was sitting down, but for some reason Cassandra didn't feel any more relaxed. There was something about this man that just didn't add up. The way he looked didn't match the other signals she was getting from him. It was like being in a room with a wild animal that, for some secret reason of its own, was pretending to be perfectly tame.

'I have a house that I'm thinking of completely modernising and redecorating,' he told her, after another of those brief but disconcerting silences. 'I've been given your name as being one of the best in your field.'

Cassandra was aware of an unexpected sense of disappointment. So, he was just another client, after all. Someone who wanted her to choose colour schemes and styles, because he didn't have the time himself—or simply couldn't be bothered.

'I'm not sure that I can take on any more commissions at the moment——' she began.

'I think that you might enjoy this one,' interrupted Jared Sinclair smoothly. 'I've recently inherited a property in Scotland, and since I don't intend to live there permanently myself, I've been considering the possibility of letting it out as a holiday home. It would require a lot of work to be done on it first, though, to get it into an acceptable condition. If I go ahead with this plan, I intend to aim at the American tourist market, which means everything will have to be brought up to a very high standard.'

Despite her firm intention not to get involved with any work for this man, Cassandra couldn't quite suppress a flicker of interest.

'Where exactly is this house? And what type of house is it? What kind of condition is it in?'

'It's in a rather remote part of the Highlands,' Jared Sinclair answered. 'Most of the house is quite old, although various alterations have been made to it over the years. It's perfectly habitable as it stands at the moment, but it certainly couldn't be advertised as first-class accommodation. It needs a professional touch to bring it up to the standard that would be required to attract American tourists.'

'Why aim at the American market?' she asked curiously.

'Because I believe it's the kind of thing which would attract them. An ancient house situated in a romantic setting——' He gave a faint smile. 'I think they'd find it irresistible—don't you?'

She had to admit he could be right. A lot of Americans had Scottish roots, and they could well be attracted by the idea of a holiday in the land of their forefathers. All the same, did she want to get involved in this sort of project?

She was surprised to find that she was actually contemplating taking it on. Just minutes ago, she had been absolutely certain that she didn't want to get involved with it. This would be a break from the usual routine, though, and the endless succession of elegant bedrooms and stylish drawing-rooms. It might even be fun.

Jared Sinclair was watching her face very closely, as if following her train of thought. He seemed a fraction more relaxed now, as if pleased that she was rather intrigued by this commission he was offering her.

'I'd need to know a lot more about it before I make a final decision,' she told him in a brisk tone.

'Of course,' he agreed instantly. 'As a matter of fact, I'm flying back to Scotland today. Why don't you come with me and take a look at the house? Then you can decide if you can cope with all the work that will be involved.'

Had it been deliberate, that note of challenge in his voice? she wondered. There had been a subtle insinuation that the job might be too big for her, that she might not be up to it. Cassandra didn't like that. She didn't need that sort of pressure, especially from someone who could already make her skin bristle by just walking into the room.

'I can't possibly come today,' she replied firmly. 'Perhaps I can fit it in one day next week——'

'It has to be today,' he interrupted calmly. 'Otherwise the whole thing's off.'

Cassandra blinked. Was he being serious? Apparently he was, because his own gaze remained perfectly steady.

'I *do* have other commitments,' she told him rather sharply.

His gaze swept over her almost empty desk. 'Do you? I had the impression that you were in the middle of a rather slack period. I don't see any reason why you can't give this job top priority.'

'Why are you in such a hurry?'

'It's already mid-autumn,' he reminded her. 'I want to get the bulk of the work done before winter sets in. Once the weather gets too severe, it'll be impossible to carry on with the work, and I want the house ready for letting out by early next spring. It'll only pay for itself if I can find tenants for the whole of the holiday season.'

That seemed to make sense. So, all she had to do now was to decide whether she wanted to take on this unexpected commission.

With some surprise, she realised that the only thing that was actually stopping her was the thought of having to work with Jared Sinclair. And she didn't know why he was having this effect on her. There was nothing about him to which she could actually object. He had been polite, reasonable, and had answered all her questions promptly and courteously. Even those strange eyes of his were now fixed on her with a bland openness, as if trying to convince her that there was nothing about him to make her nervous or afraid.

But the trouble was, he wasn't succeeding. Deep inside her, she was aware of a sense of uncertainty, an uncharacteristic edginess. She had never met

any man before who could make her feel quite like
that, and she didn't like it. It made her want to face
up to those disquieting sensations and conquer them.
And how else could she do that except by accepting
the commission this man was offering her?

'You could be back in your office by this time
tomorrow,' Jared Sinclair told her persuasively. 'It
shouldn't take you long to decide whether this job is
within your scope.'

There it was *again*, she thought with some
exasperation. That silent challenge, goading her into
proving she was up to this major task he was setting
her.

'I'm still not sure——' she began, rather stiffly.

'I had the impression that you were a very decisive
person, Miss Gregory,' he said gently. 'Why are you
finding it so hard to make up your mind about this
particular job?'

Damn it, it was almost as if he *knew* the sort of effect
he was having on her, she thought furiously. She
lifted her head and flicked back a strand of her pale
gold hair.

'In these times, a young woman would have to be
either very naïve or very stupid to go racing off into
the middle of nowhere with a man she's only just
met,' she stated coldly. 'And I'm neither of those
things.'

A smile touched the corners of his mouth, although
it didn't seem to bring any warmth to those light eyes
of his.

'I never thought for one moment that you were,
Miss Gregory.' He took out his wallet and removed a
small card. 'This is the name and phone number of
my accountant. If you ring him, he'll be pleased to
confirm that I am who I say I am. Or if you prefer

it, you can check with my bank.' He took out a gold pen. 'This is the number.'

For a moment, Cassandra hesitated. Then she picked up the phone. Why take chances?

She called the bank, and the manager was happy to confirm that Mr Jared Sinclair was indeed a customer of theirs, that he had been for several years, and that yes, he had recently acquired a property in Scotland through a rather unexpected inheritance.

Cassandra slowly put down the phone again. It all checked out. Everything seemed to be perfectly above board, which meant there was no reason why she shouldn't take a couple of days off and fly to Scotland with this man, to take a look at his house. If it proved as interesting as he had promised, it might even be what she needed to shake her out of her unexpected fit of depression.

With sudden decisiveness, she nodded. 'All right, I'll come with you.'

A look of deep satisfaction flickered across his face. Then it disappeared again so quickly that she wasn't even sure it had been there in the first place.

'Good,' he said. 'I'll pay all your initial expenses, of course, regardless of whether you finally decide to take on the job or not.' He looked at his watch. 'We should leave straight away, or we'll miss the flight. Presumably you'll want to collect some clothes first?'

'Yes. And I want to make a phone call, to let my father know where I'll be for the next couple of days.'

Jared Sinclair's dark eyebrows rose in an expression of unmistakable surprise. 'You don't still live at home do you, Miss Gregory?'

'No, I don't. I've a flat just a few minutes from

here. But I usually let my father know whenever I'm going to be out of town.' Her tone had become rather defensive now, although she couldn't figure out why. 'Is there anything very odd about that?' she added, slightly irritably.

'Not odd,' replied Jared Sinclair calmly. 'It's just that I'd have thought you were old enough to come and go without first checking in with your father.'

Cassandra flushed, something she hadn't done for years. He was making her sound as if she were a little girl instead of an independent career woman! Yet it hadn't been done offensively. She had the feeling that this man could make even the most derogatory remark sound perfectly polite and reasonable.

All the same, her hand moved away from the receiver. She could call her father some other time, when this man wasn't hovering just a couple of feet away, watching her with that cool and yet enigmatic expression.

'Do you have a car?' he asked, rising easily to his feet.

'No. Since I live so near, I walk to work.'

'Very commendable. No wonder you look so healthy.' Cassandra shot a suspicious look at him. She could have sworn there was a faintly taunting note to his voice. He was already moving towards the door, though, not giving her time to wonder about it any more. 'I've a hire car outside,' he added. 'We can use that. We'll stop off at your flat, so you can pack an overnight bag, and then we'll go straight on to the airport.'

Cassandra reached for a sheet of paper. 'I'll just leave a note for my secretary, letting her know where I've gone.' She quickly scribbled a couple of lines, and then looked up at Jared Sinclair. 'Is there any way she can get in touch with me, if something urgent comes up?'

'She can always ring you.' He dictated a phone number, which Cassandra added to the end of the note. She was relieved to learn there was a phone at his house in Scotland. It meant she could ring her father when she had a few free minutes—and when Jared Sinclair wasn't around.

Jared glanced at his watch again. 'We'd better hurry if we're going to catch that plane.'

Cassandra followed him out of the office, and she was just about to lock the outer door when Jared gave a small grunt of annoyance. 'I've left my pen on your desk.' When she went to go back into the office, he briefly laid one hand on her arm. 'It's all right, I'll fetch it.' He swiftly walked past her, not giving her time to argue. And since she remained standing by the door, she didn't see him swiftly pick up the note she had left for her secretary, crumple it into a small ball, and slide it into his pocket.

When he rejoined her, the gold pen was in his hand. 'I've got it. Let's go.'

Once they reached her flat, it took her only a few minutes to throw a few things into a bag. Since she guessed it would be a lot colder in Scotland than it was here, in London, she picked out a couple of cashmere jumpers, a slightly thicker skirt, a rather elegant little jacket in case she wanted to go out, and the necessary undies and nightwear. Zipping up the bag, she then hurried back down to the car, where Jared Sinclair was waiting for her.

They were at the airport in plenty of time to catch the flight to Inverness. After the plane had landed, Jared collected his own car from the car park, tossed

her bag into the back, and then they headed west.
During the long drive, Cassandra was vaguely aware
that they were passing through a lot of magnificent
scenery, but she didn't pay it a great deal of
attention. Lochs and mountains and rolling moorland
might appeal to a lot of people, but she definitely
preferred sun-soaked beaches and the whisper of a
warm breeze through palm trees.

After a while, she shifted rather stiffly in her seat.
'How much further?' she asked.

'We should be there in ten minutes or so,' Jared
replied. His eyes gleamed. 'Aren't you enjoying the
ride?'

'I'd enjoy it a lot more if I weren't travelling in a car
that's positively antique,' she grumbled.

In fact, her eyebrows had shot up in dismay when
she had first set eyes on it. It was a huge old black
saloon, the seats definitely designed for firmness
and hard wear instead of comfort. They had turned
off on to a poorly surfaced road a couple of miles
back, and every bump and hole—and there were
plenty of them!—seemed to be jarring a different part
of her anatomy.

'There's no point in having an expensive car
around here,' Jared said comfortably. 'You need
something sturdy that'll stand up to a lot of hard
knocks and rough weather.'

'Oh, I'm sure the car's sturdy enough,' she replied
a trifle sarcastically. 'It's *my* chassis that isn't
designed to take all this jolting.'

His gaze briefly slid over her. 'You might not be
built for endurance, but it would be hard to improve
on the overall design,' he commented.

Cassandra instantly shot a dark frown in his
direction. He could cut out that sort of remark right

now! She was here to work, and that was all. If Jared Sinclair had any other ideas, he had better forget them—and fast.

He didn't say another word, though. Nor did he show any further sign of interest in her. Cassandra bounced around uncomfortably on her seat for a couple more minutes, then she turned round and frowned at him again.

'Why has the road suddenly got so bad?' she asked rather crossly.

'It's a private road,' he replied. 'Along with most of the land around here, it belongs to the estate.'

'Well, if you want to attract tourists here, you'll have to improve the road as well as the house.'

'Will I?'

His slightly ambiguous answer bothered her a little. In fact, she was ready to admit that there was quite a lot about this man that bothered her. Something wasn't—quite right. She couldn't explain it to herself any clearer than that; it was just a gut feeling that was growing stronger by the minute.

So, why had she ever agreed to come to this remote place with him? Probably because she was feeling in a rather perverse mood at the moment, Cassandra told herself wryly. And anyway, she hated to admit that she couldn't handle any situation—or anyone. Call it pride, or just plain stubbornness. Either way, she wasn't going to run away from a job just because her nerves felt unexpectedly twitchy!

The road was running alongside a long, narrow loch now. The landscape looked wild and desolate, with mountains rearing up in the background, their peaks wreathed in heavy cloud. There were a few isolated clumps of pine, a lot of rocky outcrops, and great patches of heather, its colour fading as autumn advanced. Perhaps it all looked better when the sun was shining, Cassandra decided rather gloomily. If not, Jared Sinclair was in trouble. Surely no one would want to come and look at this sombre view for days on end?

Half a mile further on, the road swung round to the right, turning away from the loch and climbing steadily. Despite its age, the car coped easily with the steep gradient. On the outside, it might look just about ready for the scrap yard, but the engine purred smoothly under the rather rusty bonnet, and seemed capable of surprising bursts of speed.

Cassandra didn't see the house straight away. Its stonework was so dark that it seemed to merge in with the heavy shadows cast by the stand of tall pines just behind it. When her eyes finally picked it out, she gave an inward groan. It might be romantic, but it certainly wasn't very beautiful! Bits added on here and there, with no thought for the overall design, old-fashioned sash windows, tiles which were a depressing shade of grey, and a jumble of outbuildings which littered the unkempt patch of garden.

'Is this it?' she said unenthusiastically, as Jared began to slow the car.

'This is it,' he agreed. 'Don't you think it has possibilities?'

Was he teasing her—or taunting her? It was impossible to be sure. Seconds later, the car had stopped outside the front entrance and Jared was getting out.

'Aren't you going to come inside?' he invited, holding open the car door for her.

Quite suddenly, Cassandra knew that was the very last thing she wanted to do. She didn't have much choice, though. They were miles from anywhere—there was nowhere else she *could* go. Comforting herself with the thought that she could ring for a taxi and head straight back to the airport if things were too grim, she swung herself out of the car and carefully picked her way along the uneven path that led to the front door. Perhaps high heels weren't a very practical form of footwear for the Highlands! she thought to herself ruefully.

Jared opened the front door and stepped inside. With a small grimace, she followed him into the house. Her heels clicked noisily on the stone-flagged floor, and she could almost feel the cold rising up from it. Already, she was shivering. Anyone living here for more than a couple of days would need a complete set of thermal underwear!

Things didn't improve. What little furniture there was looked old and strictly functional. They passed through a large hall which had a beamed ceiling, bare walls, and a large fireplace packed with logs. Cassandra wished the fire was lit. She had only been in the house a couple of minutes and she was already freezing.

A little further on there was a drawing-room, which looked just a fraction more comfortable. There was a heavy sofa in front of the fireplace, and from the windows Cassandra could see a fairly spectacular view of the loch and the mountains. Fine—if you liked that sort of thing, she thought to herself with a fresh wave of depression.

She decided she had already seen enough. Through open doorways, she had glimpsed the other rooms on the ground floor, and it wasn't difficult to come to an instant conclusion. It would take a small fortune to transform this place into the sort of holiday

home that Jared Sinclair had in mind. It wasn't worth
it. It would take years to recoup the capital sum he
would have to lay out.

She decided she might as well tell him so straight
away, and save them both a lot of time and trouble.
With luck, he would offer to drive her back to
Inverness, and she could catch a late flight back to
London.

When she turned to face him, though, she found
his features had altered dramatically in the last few
seconds. It was as if a mask had slid away, at last
letting her see what lay underneath.

And Cassandra didn't like what she was seeing.
The quicksilver eyes seemed to hold a glow of
triumph, his mouth was set in a new and hard line,
and all trace of blandness had disappeared.

With an effort, she pushed her deep unease to one
side. 'I think it's time we had a talk,' she said briskly.
'This house of yours—it's not exactly Shangri-La, is
it?'

'No, it isn't,' he agreed softly. 'But it suits my
purpose very well.'

'Your purpose?' she echoed edgily.

Jared leant back against the heavy stone mantel-
piece behind him. 'Do you think it'll make an ideal
holiday home?' he goaded, and there was no
mistaking the mockery in his voice now. 'Do you
recommend that I spend a great deal of money
turning it into a luxury residence?'

'No, I don't,' she replied bluntly. 'And I'm
beginning to think that you never had the slightest
intention of doing any such thing.'

'Clever girl,' he applauded her. 'But then, you
come from a clever family, Miss Cassandra Gregory. I
believe your father is regarded as an absolutely

brilliant businessman.'

'My father's certainly very successful,' she retorted, nerves now making her voice sharp. 'But I don't see what that's got to do with you.'

'Of course you don't,' he said, his mouth relaxing into one of the most unpleasant smiles she had ever seen. 'If you did, you'd never have come here with me.'

Something about his tone made her take a couple of steps back from him. Annoyed at her sudden cowardice, she forced herself to stand still again. She didn't know what this was about—but she had the feeling that she was very soon going to find out.

'There's one question that you never asked me,' Jared Sinclair went on in that same low, hard voice. 'You weren't interested in knowing if this house had a name.'

'And does it?'

'Oh, yes. It's called Glenveil.'

As soon as he said it, she knew she had heard that name before. But where? She hunted back through her memory, but it was hard to think straight with those light eyes fixed on her so unwaveringly.

'Need a little help?' he offered. 'Try Glenveil Toys—it's the name of a company that your father acquired a few months ago.'

She was still struggling to recall the details, though. 'Yes, I think I remember,' she said slowly, with a small frown. 'I was working so hard at the time, though, getting my own business going. I didn't pay much attention to anything else that was going on. Didn't the company get into financial difficulties? Then my father took it over, to stop it going bankrupt?'

Jared Sinclair's eyes suddenly burned. 'It got into

financial difficulties because your father had enough
power and influence to create that situation! He
persuaded creditors to demand instant payment, cut
off supplies of finance, spread rumours about the
company being unstable so that customers backed off
from signing new contracts. And he chose exactly the
right time to launch his attack, a period when the
company was vulnerable. Glenveil Toys was basically
sound, though. If there hadn't been any outside
interference from your father, there wouldn't have
been any problems.'

Automatically, she jumped to her father's defence.
She always did. 'My father would never do anything
so underhand,' she stated coldly. 'Anyway, who told
you all this?'

'No one had to tell me,' Jared replied grimly.
'Glenveil Toys was *my* company. I spent ten years
building it up. Everything I had, everything I'd
worked for, was tied up in it. If I'd lost it through my
own incompetence, I could just about have lived with
that. But I didn't. I lost it because your father used
every devious trick he could to cheat me out of it.'

'I don't believe you!' Her nerves were jumping
now, but she still managed to keep her voice staunch
and steady.

'I really don't care if you believe me or not. It
happens to be the truth. My God, I should know!'

Cassandra saw him make an effort to keep his fast-
flaring temper under control, and she shivered. The
man was mad! Saying all those terrible things about
her father, putting the blame on him because Jared
Sinclair wasn't man enough to admit that his
company had failed because of his own mismanage-
ment.

'We can argue about this all day and not come to

any agreement,' she said, deliberately keeping her own voice calm, even though she was quivering inside. 'If you've brought me here to try and convince me that my father's a—well, a crook, it's just not going to work, I'm afraid.'

Jared's gaze suddenly glittered. 'But that isn't why I brought you here at all,' he told her silkily. He paused, as if relishing the situation, enjoying a few moments of triumph after a long, long wait. 'I never thought I was the sort of man who would deliberately go out looking for revenge. But these last few months, I've found out quite a few things about myself that I never knew before—and not all of them pleasant,' he added, with a brief darkening of his eyes.

'What——' Cassandra swallowed hard. 'What do you mean? What are you going to do to me?'

'Do to you?' he repeated. 'If you're talking about physical harm—nothing at all.' Before she had time to relax, though, he went on, 'But I *do* have certain plans for you.'

'What sort of plans?' she got out through teeth that had infuriatingly begun to chatter, letting him know exactly how on edge she was.

'Do you know what hurts people most of all?' Jared said, answering her question with one of his own. 'It's losing someone—or something—that you love or deeply value. Because of your father, I lost my company. It seemed only fair to me that he should lose something in return—even if it's only temporary. So I began to look at the possibilities. His wife? But he never remarried after your mother died. Which left his daughter. His only child, whom he's spoilt and doted on since the day she was born. Cassandra Gregory—who's now here, in my house.' A look of perverse satisfaction crossed his face. 'And who'll stay here until I decide to let her leave.'

Cassandra was getting to the stage where she didn't believe any of this was really happening.

'If you think you can keep me here against my will, it won't work,' she threw at him with a fresh burst of defiance. 'My secretary knows where I am. She'll let everyone know where they can find me.'

Jared reached into his pocket and took out a crumpled sheet of paper. 'I'm afraid not,' he said regretfully. 'I removed your note from her desk before we left your office.'

'This is crazy,' she muttered shakily. '*You're* crazy.'

'I don't think so. Not that it's really important. At least, not to me.'

'Well, it's sure as hell important to me,' she retorted. 'Being kidnapped by someone who's having some sort of brainstorm——'

Jared merely smiled. She had to admit that he looked perfectly sane. And everything he had said made an awful kind of sense, if he truly believed her father capable of the devious and ruthless behaviour of which he had accused him.

'Call it a brainstorm if you like,' he said calmly. 'It doesn't worry me. In fact, very little worries me these days. And it won't change anything. Your father's about to learn what it's like to lose the thing of most value in his life. As far as he's concerned, for the next few days it's going to be as if his daughter's disappeared off the very face of the earth!'

CHAPTER TWO

JARED SINCLAIR left her on her own after that, as if he wanted to give her time to take in everything he had told her. Cassandra had only one thought in her head, though. Getting away from here! She didn't intend to be kept a prisoner by someone who was clearly out of his mind.

A quick exploration of the other rooms on the ground floor confirmed her suspicions. There was no phone; there had probably never been any phone. Jared Sinclair had lied about that, just as he had lied about so many other things—including the way in which her father had acquired Glenveil Toys.

She gave a small shrug. If she couldn't telephone for help, then there was no alternative. She would have to walk out of here.

A glance out of the window told her it had started to rain. Cassandra frowned, but wasn't deterred. All right, she would get wet!

She pulled on her light jacket, peered cautiously round to see if there was any sign of Jared Sinclair, and then quietly let herself out of the front door. The path was uneven and difficult to negotiate in high heels, but she persevered, walking as fast as she dared. A couple of times, she turned and glanced back at the house, but there was still no sign of Jared. He didn't seem to have realised she had gone, which gave her some satisfaction. She hadn't thought it would be this easy to get away.

Once she reached the road, she looked quickly in both directions, trying to decide which way to go. Were there any houses nearby, where she could go for help? She certainly couldn't see any, although it was difficult to see very far in the steadily increasing rain. Quickly, she hunted back through her memory, trying to remember if she had seen any farms or houses during the last stage of their drive up here. With a definite sinking sensation in the pit of her stomach, she had to admit that she hadn't noticed any. In fact, one thing which had struck her was the sheer emptiness of this part of the Highlands. It was as if it had hardly been touched by human habitation.

Well, perhaps there were some houses ahead, she told herself with forced optimism. But, unless she hurried, she would never have a chance to find out. Surely it wouldn't be long before Jared Sinclair realised she was missing, and came after her?

However, it was impossible to walk quickly in high heels, and the road surface was far too rough to let her walk barefooted. Why on earth hadn't she packed some sensible, flat-soled shoes? Because she hadn't known that Jared Sinclair was a madman, and that he planned to hold her a prisoner in this awful place! she muttered in a sudden burst of edgy temper mixed with angry frustration.

The rain had begun to pour down now. In minutes, she was drenched to the skin and freezing cold, and her shoes were rubbing sore blisters on her heels. She stubbornly kept going, though. *Nothing* would have induced her to go back to that cold, comfortless house, and Jared Sinclair.

She had absolutely no idea how long she kept walking. It had to have been over an hour, she decided wearily as she trudged on through the heavy drizzle. And the really odd thing was that Jared hadn't come after her. Perhaps he had never really meant to keep her shut away in that house. Maybe just luring her up here and scaring her half to death had been enough for him, and he was satisfied with that.

A couple of minutes later, a dark shaped loomed up in front of her. Cassandra blinked, and then let out a weary sigh of relief. A cottage! She had made it. In just a few minutes, she would be warm and dry, and sending a message to her father to come and rescue her from this nightmare.

She hobbled up the overgrown path to the front door, and then hammered on it loudly. When no one opened it, she hammered again, and then stood back impatiently, peering up at the windows to see if she could see any sign of life.

With a nasty jolt of her nerve-ends, she noticed what she had been too preoccupied to notice before. Several panes of glass were either cracked or broken, and the cottage had a distinctly derelict air about it.

Although she knocked on the door a couple more times, it was without any real hope. She tried peering in through the downstairs windows, but they were too grimy to let her see inside. It was pretty obvious that she was out of luck, though. The cottage was uninhabited.

A great wave of depression swept over her. Her legs ached, her feet were sore and raw where her wet shoes had chafed her skin, and she was so freezing cold that she didn't think she would ever be able to get warm again. For the first time since she was a child, Cassandra wanted to sit down and just cry from sheer misery.

Instead, she turned round and began to drag herself wearily back down the path. And that was when she noticed the large black car parked on the road, just a few yards away.

Somehow, she wasn't at all surprised to see it. At the back of her mind, she had known all along that Jared Sinclair had never had any intention of letting her go.

She walked over to the car and stared down at him coldly. 'Come to gloat?' she enquired, hating him so deeply at that moment that she was sure he must be able to see the pure venom in her eyes.

He merely opened the car door for her. 'Get in,' he ordered.

'Thanks for the offer, but I prefer to walk!'

'Don't be stupid!' He leaned over, gripped hold of her arm, and pulled her into the car. From the moment Cassandra felt his fingers on her arm, she knew it was useless to struggle. This man was strong—mugh stronger than she had expected. If it came to a physical tussle between them, there was no doubt in her mind who would win.

They drove back to Glenveil in silence, and as they pulled up in front of the house Cassandra found herself hating it more than ever.

'This place is awful!' she muttered. 'How on earth can you stand to live here?'

Jared merely shrugged. 'I never really think about it.'

'Don't you *care?*' she said a little incredulously.

'Not particularly.' He got out of the car and strode towards the house, not even looking to see if she was following him.

The last thing in the world that Cassandra wanted

to do was to trail after him into that cold mausoleum of a place. She was just too frozen and exhausted, though, for any pointless gestures of defiance.

Jared headed towards the drawing-room and, reluctantly, she followed. Then she was glad that she had, because she found the fire had been lit. The logs were spitting and crackling as they burnt brightly, and she instantly made for the warm glow.

As she huddled over the flames, she turned her head and glowered at him.

'How did you know where to find me?'

'It wasn't difficult,' he replied. 'I was watching from the window when you left the house, so I saw which way you went. I knew it would take you about an hour to reach the cottage. All I had to do was wait for a while, and then come in the car to pick you up.'

'You think you're so damned clever, don't you?' she muttered angrily. 'Anyway, why did you let me go so far in that pouring rain? You could have come after me straight away, and saved me from getting soaked and frozen.'

'Yes, I could,' he agreed coolly. 'But I wanted you to find out for yourself just how hard it is to get away from here. In the direction you went, the road doesn't go any further than that derelict cottage. If you try and go the other way, you'll walk nearly fifteen miles before you see any sign of a house. And before you've gone even half that distance, I'll have come after you and brought you back here again.'

'All right,' she snapped, 'there's no need to rub it in. You've made it perfectly clear. There's almost no way I can get away from this place. So—how long do you intend to keep me here?'

'I haven't decided yet,' he answered calmly.

Cassandra glared at him in frustration. For so much of her life, men had dictated what she could or couldn't do. No, not men, she corrected herself rather guiltily. One man—her father. He had done it through love, of course, so she supposed that ought to make a difference. Yet, somehow, the feeling of being trapped had been just the same. And, just when she thought she was beginning to break free a little, Jared Sinclair had come along with his own very distinctive brand of imprisonment.

It was intolerable, she told herself fiercely. She was beginning to feel as if she hated all men, for the power they had over her, and the physical strength that enabled them to maintain that dominance. To have someone like Jared step in and take over her life like this, restricting her movements, giving orders which he clearly expected to be obeyed—she wouldn't, *couldn't* stand for it.

'You do realise what'll happen when I finally get out of here?' she told him furiously. 'You'll be charged with kidnapping. You'll go to gaol. And I hope they keep you there until you rot!'

Jared Sinclair seemed totally unperturbed by her outburst. 'I haven't kidnapped you,' he reminded her. 'At least, not technically speaking. I'm not demanding money in return for your release.'

'I very much doubt if the courts will look at it like that,' she retorted. 'One way or another, you'll pay for this.'

He merely shrugged. 'Perhaps I will.' He didn't appear in the least concerned by the prospect.

Cassandra stared at him in growing bafflement. 'It really doesn't worry you, does it?' she said slowly, at last.

'No, it doesn't,' he agreed. 'Although it might

worry me a little if you become ill through sitting
around for too long in wet clothes. I told you that I
don't intend you to come to any physical harm, and I
meant it. You'd better go and find something dry to
wear.'

'I'm so cold,' she complained. 'Even putting on dry
clothes isn't going to make much difference. About
the only thing that'll get me warm is a long soak in a
very hot bath.' She stared at him belligerently. 'I
suppose this house does have proper plumbing?' she
demanded.

'Yes, it does. But I'm afraid the boiler isn't lit. There
isn't any hot water.'

'No hot water?' she repeated in disbelief. 'Oh, this
is ridiculous!'

'The boiler needs clearing out,' Jared said with
unexpected patience. 'I'll do it in the morning.
There'll be hot water by tomorrow lunch time.'

'And I'm supposed to wait for a bath until then?'
She didn't care that her voice was cracking a little
now. She had had enough of this place, this man,
this entire absurd situation.

'There's an old tin bath somewhere,' Jared told her.
'If you like, I'll bring it in here, heat up some water
on the stove, and you can use that.'

'A tin bath in front of the fire?' She wanted to
laugh, but was suddenly afraid that she might end up
with a very different kind of tears filling her eyes.
'Oh, what the hell,' she muttered in sudden defeat.
'I'll do *anything* to get warm.'

'Go upstairs and change into something dry while
I'm heating up the water,' he instructed. 'I've put
your things in the bedroom at the top of the stairs.'

Loath to leave the fire, but at the same time
wanting to get out of the wet clothes that were cling-

ing damply to her chilled skin, Cassandra moved towards the door. Jared was standing on the far side of the room, his face shadowed now as evening began to draw in. She looked at him for several long moments, then she shook her head.

'I'm still not convinced that I'm not dreaming all of this,' she said, rather bemusedly.

His mouth curled into a not entirely pleasant smile. 'Believe me, the whole thing's very real.'

She stared at him for a while longer. 'Yes, I'm beginning to realise that,' she said at last, in a quiet voice. Then she turned away from that tall, shadowed figure, and left the room.

She found her bedroom without any difficulty. Her overnight bag had been tossed on to the bed—a fourposter, she noted with wry amusement. Maybe this house *did* have one or two romantic touches. Shivering deeply now, she stripped off her soaked clothes and then pulled on the spare jumper and skirt she had brought with her. It didn't make very much difference, she was still chilled to the bone. Guessing that it would take some time to heat up enough water for her bath, she sat on the edge of the bed and pulled the quilt around her shoulders for extra warmth as she waited.

Some time later, there was a brief knock on the door. 'Your bath's ready,' Jared informed her, rather curtly.

It was getting dark now. As she walked over to the door, she clicked down the light switch, but nothing happened. She opened the door and found Jared still standing outside.

'Hey,' she said, a little alarmed. 'What's happened to the electricity?'

'We're not connected to the mains,' replied Jared.

'All our power comes from a small generator.'

She gave an exaggerated groan. 'Let me guess—
you haven't got it going yet. Is that something else
that's going to have to wait until the morning?'

'We can easily manage for one night without
proper heat or light,' he told her in an unperturbed
tone.

'You might not mind living like a Spartan, but I'm
used to a rather more comfortable life,' she
grumbled. 'How can I take a bath in the dark?'

'There are plenty of candles.'

'*Candles*? Oh, great! Things are just getting better
and better!' she said rudely.

He didn't react to her rudeness, though. 'You'd
better take your bath before the water gets cold,' was
all he said.

Cassandra thought she detected a sudden note of
tiredness in his voice. She narrowed her eyes, trying
to see his face clearly, but the shadows were too thick
now. He was little more than a dark silhouette. She
gave a small shrug. She hoped he *was* tired. In fact,
she hoped that lugging all that hot water round to fill
her bath had left him completely wiped out. It was
certainly no more than he deserved, considering his
appalling behaviour.

She made her way back downstairs, and found that
an old-fashioned tin bath had been set out on the rug
in front of the fire, in the drawing-room. Several
candles had been lit and placed around the room,
giving an illusion of warmth and comfort as they gave
off a mellow glow. Cassandra wasn't deceived,
though. There wasn't any real warmth in this house.
And, even if there had been, Jared Sinclair would
have quickly destroyed it with the cold aura of his
personality.

She closed the door, looked to see if it had a lock on it, and was disappointed to find that it hadn't. With a resigned shrug, she walked over to the bath, stripped off her clothes, and then gingerly stepped into it.

The water was certainly hot! The only trouble was, there wasn't much of it; just a few inches in the bottom. Cassandra, who liked to wallow in a bath filled almost to the brim and liberally laced with expensive scent, gave a small sigh and tried to make the best of it. It was cramped, too; she had to sit with her knees drawn nearly up to her chin. At least the combination of hot water and warm fire was beginning to thaw her out a little, though. Half an hour of this, and she might begin to feel half-way human again.

As the water finally began to cool, she regretfully decided it was time to get out. And it was then that she realised that she didn't have a towel.

She muttered frustratedly under her breath. By the time she had dripped her way wetly upstairs, to fetch the one in her bag, she would be as cold as when she had first got into the bath. Anyway, there was no way she was going to walk through the house totally naked. Jared Sinclair might seem to be outwardly fairly unemotional, but now and then she had caught glimpses of an inner turbulence which had definitely disturbed her. After all, he *had* to be unstable, or he would never have gone ahead with this insane plan to keep her a prisoner here. With a man in that sort of mental state, you could never be sure of what he was going to do next—or how he was going to react.

Since there wasn't any real alternative, she decided she would just have to sit by the fire until she was reasonably dry. She was about to haul herself out of the bath when the door opened and Jared strolled in.

'Haven't you ever heard of knocking?' she enquired with an angry edginess. At the same time, she hurriedly slid as deep down in the bath as she could get.

'I thought you might need these,' Jared replied, without much interest. He tossed a couple of towels over to her, expertly aiming them so that they landed only a few inches away from the bath.

'Thanks,' she muttered, although there wasn't much trace of gratitude in her voice. Moving very carefully, she reached out just one arm and picked up the nearest towel. As her fingers sank into the soft towelling, she raised her eyebrows in feigned surprise. 'I didn't expect this sort of luxury. Considering the way things have gone so far, I thought you'd probably expect me to rub myself dry on lengths of coarse cotton!'

'I wouldn't want you to think that I'm totally uncivilised.' His response was smooth and definitely mocking. Cassandra instantly bristled in response.

'Do you think anyone in their right mind would describe your behaviour as *civilised*?'

'It seems perfectly reasonable to me.'

'Then you've got a very weird idea of what is and isn't reasonable,' she retorted. 'For instance, most people would have knocked before they came in. And they certainly wouldn't just stand there, watching me take my bath!'

Jared remained unruffled. And that disturbed Cassandra more than anything. She wasn't used to men being indifferent to her. One way or another, they always reacted—and usually fairly strongly!

His light gaze was still resting on her, and she could have sworn she caught a glint of amusement in the depth of those silver eyes. It was hard to be sure, since the candles didn't give off enough brightness to see anything very clearly, but she had a strong suspicion that he was laughing at her. Except that this man didn't seem to laugh at anything, she reminded herself uneasily. He rarely even smiled, and when he did it was with very little trace of genuine humour.

Cassandra gave a small shiver, and wasn't at all certain that it was because the water in the bath had lost much of its heat by now.

'I'd appreciate it if you'd leave, and let me get dried and dressed,' she said stiffly.

'Such politeness,' he mocked softly. 'Why don't you just tell me to get out?'

'Because I've tried rudeness, and it doesn't work,' came her tense retort. 'I thought I'd try a little courtesy for a change, and see if that got any results. Obviously, it doesn't make the slightest bit of difference,' she went on, flinging an angry glance at him. 'You intend to be as objectionable as possible. You're really getting a kick out of keeping me here, aren't you? You do realise it's sick? A really disgusting way of getting a cheap thrill?'

This time, she finally got a response. Jared strode further into the room, grabbed one of the towels, and flung it at her.

'Wrap that round you,' he ordered.

She stared at him apprehensively. 'Why?'

'Because I want you out of that bath. And *now.*'

Cassandra's eyes flashed at him. 'Are you sure you want me to bother with the towel?' she taunted.

His brief flare of temper had passed, though. His tone was perfectly cool again when he answered her.

'Personally, I don't give a damn if you're stark

naked, or clothed from head to toe. But if you're not out of that bath in five seconds, I'll drag you out myself.'

Remembering how strong his fingers had felt when they had gripped her earlier, and pulled her into his car, Cassandra resentfully obeyed. Right at this moment, she fiercely loathed this man for taking away her independence, her freedom of choice. He was making her feel like a young child who had no option except to obey the orders of an all-powerful adult.

Holding the towel in front of her like a screen, she managed to get out of the bath without showing more than a few inches of bare arms and legs. Then she fastened it firmly under her arms, and was grateful that it was long enough to hide virtually her whole body.

She lifted her head and stared at Jared defiantly. 'What now?'

'A little demonstration—just to put your mind at rest.'

'What kind of demonstration?' There was a definite note of wariness in her voice now.

'Just something to convince you that you'll be perfectly safe, no matter how long I decide to keep you here.'

He came a step closer, and she instantly backed away.

'Frightened of me?' he taunted quietly. 'But that's what this is all about, Cassandra. To prove to you that you don't have any grounds for those kind of fears.'

She still kept backing away, though.

'Stay where you are,' Jared ordered.

To her amazement, she instantly obeyed. What on

earth was the matter with her? she wondered, with a first touch of confusion. Why was she beginning to feel an awful compulsion to do exactly as this man instructed?

Jared moved forward again, so that he was standing only inches away from her. His silver gaze ran over her objectively, and it was quite impossible to guess what he was thinking.

'You're a very beautiful girl, Cassandra,' he said at last. There was no inflection in his voice, though, no trace of any recognisable emotion. He might have been talking about some statue that he found aesthetically pleasing, but which didn't move him in any other way.

'I've been told that before,' she replied evenly. It was true. She wasn't a vain girl, but she knew perfectly well that her combination of pale gold hair and violet eyes always drew male attention. Her thin, elegant body was an extra bonus. Dressed or undressed, she always looked good. Sometimes it was an asset, and sometimes it was a nuisance, drawing a lot of unwanted male attention.

Was that what was going to happen now? she wondered uneasily. And yet, strangely, although Jared was standing so close and studying her with blatant openness, she didn't feel any real sense of threat.

'Quite a few men must have kissed you,' he remarked.

'I don't see that's any of your damn business,' she flared back at him.

'I think that it is, since you're obviously expecting me to do exactly the same.'

'I am *not*——'

'Yes, you are,' Jared replied calmly. 'So perhaps

it would be better to get it over and done with, right
now——'

He had barely finished speaking before he moved
forward and covered her lips with his own.
Cassandra briefly flinched at their coolness, and then
started to struggle. His touch was firm, though, and
after an unexpectedly short time she became still
again, telling herself that she might as well let him do
what he wanted, and be done with it as quickly as
possible. Her own submissiveness astounded her.
She usually retaliated quite savagely when men came
on to her against her will. She couldn't stand being
mauled, and had been to self-defence classes to learn
several painful ways of making sure that they backed
off again pretty quickly.

With Jared Sinclair, though, she simply stood there
as his mouth moved over hers, exploring in an almost
disinterested manner. One of his hands rested lightly
on her shoulder, as if to steady her, but apart from
that he wasn't touching her. His breathing remained
steady, his skin was cool, and she had the distinct
impression that he was finding the whole thing about
as arousing as brushing his teeth.

To her alarm, she found that *she* was the one who
was beginning to get flustered. There was an odd
tightness in her chest, her legs were starting to feel
shaky, and there was a growing warmth in the pit of
her stomach.

Before she had time to get into a total panic over her
reaction, though, Jared had lifted his head and
moved back from her.

'Get the message?' he said, in a conversational
tone. 'I'm not interested. You don't have to lock your
door against me, or run away when you see me
coming. You're not in any danger from any kind of

sexual assault.'

Cassandra still found it hard to believe. Men had *always* been interested in her, ever since her early teens. Jared was already walking away, though, leaving her standing there with a lot of very confused thoughts rushing through her head.

It wasn't until he had actually left the room that she found herself able to think clearly again. And, once her head started to straighten itself out, she was quite appalled at the way she had reacted. Had he noticed? Worse than that, had he got the impression that she was actually interested in him? Oh, God, she hoped not! That really would be the final humiliation.

She was tired, she told herself a little desperately. That was all. It had been a long day—and a crazy day. In the morning, she would feel more like herself again. And she would definitely find some way of getting away from here. She didn't intend to sit meekly around until Jared finally deigned to let her go.

Her legs still feeling infuriatingly weak, she slowly made her way upstairs to her room. It felt like an icebox. Wishing she had packed warm pyjamas instead of a cotton nightie, she quickly undressed and jumped into bed, shivering as the cold sheets touched her skin.

The rain was still pelting against the windows, and the wind was rising now, making the ill-fitting frames rattle. Oh, great! she thought to herself irritably. It was just what her frayed nerves needed.

Then, through all the other sounds, came one which was quite unmistakable. The sharp click of a lock, as a key was turned.

Cassandra immediately sat up in bed and stared at the door. Surely he wouldn't dare——? She quickly pushed back the sheets, and padded over to the door. One turn of the handle was enough to confirm that she hadn't imagined it. He had locked her in!

Furiously, she rattled the handle, and then banged on the door itself. 'Damn it, you can't *do* this!' she yelled angrily.

There was no reply, and she guessed he had gone straight back to his own room. She could shout and thump on the door all night, but it wouldn't make the slightest difference. No one would hear her, and no one would come to let her out.

She trailed back to bed, filled with disbelief that all of this was actually happening to her, Cassandra Gregory. Although totally drained by the incredible events of the day, she found it impossible to sleep. She dozed fitfully a couple of times, but kept being woken up again by the rattling window-frames, or the howling of the wind through the pine trees behind the house. And a couple of times she thought she could hear someone coughing. Jared? She supposed it had to be, because he was the only other person in the house. Good, she thought savagely, she hoped he had caught his death of a cold out in that rain this afternoon!

Towards dawn, she finally slid into a deeper sleep. When she dreamed, though, it was of Jared Sinclair's kiss, and she moved restlessly in the bed for a while before finally becoming still again, and sleeping peacefully until late in the morning.

CHAPTER THREE

WHEN she opened her eyes, Cassandra was astonished to find the room filled with sunshine. Blinking a little in the bright light, she crawled out of bed and went over to look out of the window.

The sky was a bright and beautiful blue, the water of the loch sparkled, and, instead of being grey and rainswept, the mountains were mottled with gorgeous shades of green and russet. With her eye for colour, Cassandra could appreciate the subtle hues, and the darker dapplings of amethyst from the irregular patches of fading heather.

'A definite improvement on yesterday,' she murmured to herself. 'A few more days like this, and I might even get to like it around here.'

Then she remembered everything that had happened yesterday—remembered the final ignominy of being locked in her room last night—and her face darkened again. While she was being kept here against her will, there was no way she would ever look on this place favourably.

Was she still locked in? she wondered. There was only one way to find out. She went over to the door, tried it, and found that it opened immediately. Cassandra scowled. It didn't alter the fact that it had been locked last night, shutting her in like some naughty schoolgirl who had to be punished.

Quickly she dressed, and then brushed the pale, straight fall of her hair. She was still angry. On top of that, though, she was also starving hungry. She couldn't remember when she had last eaten.

She made her way down to the kitchen, and even as she opened the door the delicious smell of bacon cooking wafted towards her. Jared was standing at the stove, expertly breaking eggs into a pan. As she came in, he glanced round.

'Hungry?'

'Yes,' she said, hating to admit it. Then, not forgetting her main grievance, she rounded on him. 'How *dared* you lock me in my room last night?'

'I didn't want you wandering off in the middle of the night and getting lost in the mountains,' he replied calmly. 'They're treacherous enough in the daytime, let alone after dark.'

'I wouldn't do anything that stupid.'

'Wouldn't you? I got the impression that you were so determined to get away from here that you'd take just about any risk. It was for your own safety that I locked you in.'

'And do you intend to do the same thing *every* night?' she demanded. 'For my own safety, of course,' she added with heavy sarcasm.

'That rather depends.'

'On what?'

'On whether you'll give me your word that you won't leave the house after dark.'

'Of course I will,' she said promptly, telling herself that she needn't feel any compunction about breaking any promises she made to this man.

His gaze rested on her thoughtfully. 'But can I trust you to keep that promise? You are a Gregory.'

Cassandra's eyes became cold. 'And what's that supposed to mean?'

'I just wondered if you'd inherited many of your

father's less pleasant traits,' he replied, in that same cool voice. 'Including the capacity to lie through your teeth whenever it suits you.'

'My father doesn't lie!'

'Then we don't seem to be talking about the same man,' came Jared's hard reply. 'Because the Randolph Gregory that I knew would lie, cheat and blackmail without a moment's compunction.'

Scorn instantly showed in Cassandra's violet-blue gaze. 'I don't believe you. And I think it's a pretty disgusting thing to do, blaming someone else because you were too inefficient, too incompetent, to keep your business going!'

More than anything else she had ever said to him, that seemed to strike a raw nerve. The quicksilver eyes blazed into sudden life, his entire body tensed, and he actually took a couple of steps forward before he seemed to realise what he was doing, and stood still again.

He took a deep breath, and gradually the light in his eyes died away, leaving the unemotional expression to which she had become accustomed.

'You should be very grateful that I'm not a violent man,' he told her in a voice that was completely under control again now.

'Not violent?' she scoffed. 'Then what do you call what you've done to me these last twenty-four hours?'

'Have you been hurt in any way?' he challenged immediately. 'Have I done anything to physically injure you?'

For some reason, she found herself remembering that kiss he had given her last night. Didn't that count as an injury? she told herself rebelliously. Forcing himself on her like that? Yet, for some reason, she stopped herself from saying it out loud. After all, she excused herself reluctantly, he hadn't actually been rough. And he certainly hadn't tried to take it any further than that one kiss.

'There are different ways of hurting people,' she muttered at last.

An icy smile touched the corners of Jared's mouth. 'I'm glad that you understand that,' he said softly.

'Oh, yes, I forgot,' she said, with some bitterness. 'You're trying to hurt my father—through me.'

'It seemed the most effective way,' he agreed.

'And it doesn't matter that *I'm* suffering, as well? And all because of something that's nothing to do with me, that isn't even my fault?'

'You know the old saying about "the sins of the fathers",' Jared reminded her. 'And it doesn't seem to me that you're suffering too badly. Your pride's taken a bit of a knock, of course. And since you've always been pampered, you're not enjoying the fact that you're having to put up with a few physical discomforts. But suffering? No, Miss Cassandra Gregory, I don't think that anyone could say that you were actually suffering,' he finished, a trifle grimly.

'Then what am I meant to do?' she demanded. 'Look on this as some sort of holiday?'

He shrugged. 'That's entirely up to you. You can make the best of the situation, or you can sit in your room and sulk all day. It makes no difference to me.'

'You really are incredible,' she said, with a disbelieving shake of her head. 'And what exactly are you getting out of this pathetic little charade?'

'Justice,' he said simply. 'A sense of justice.'

'And are you enjoying it?' came her contemptuous reply.

'No, I'm not enjoying it,' he answered in an expressionless voice. 'I find there's very little that actually gives me any pleasure these days, but I am getting a certain sense of satisfaction.'

'Satisfaction? Or revenge?' she challenged.

' "Revenge is a kind of wild justice",' he quoted back at her. 'I want your father to know exactly what it feels like to lose something of irreplaceable value. Do you think he's beginning to miss you by now?' he goaded softly. 'Do you suppose he's already begun to worry, made efforts to try and find out where you are?'

Cassandra knew that it was entirely possible. Her father was in touch most days, on the phone if not in person. When he found she wasn't at her office, he would immediately ring her flat. And when he didn't get any reply there——

'This whole thing's sick,' she said, in a suddenly helpless voice. 'What kind of man are you, to do something like this?'

'Perhaps I've turned into the same kind of man as your father,' answered Jared with a cruel smile. 'Wouldn't that be a fine joke, if we finally had something in common?'

'I'm not laughing,' she flung back at him in a choked voice.

'And neither was I, when I lost my company,' he said, his tone abruptly changing and taking on a dark note that sent an icy quiver right down her spine. 'Nor were all the others who lost their companies in exactly the same way.'

That made her lift her head sharply. 'What others?'

'Did you think that was the first time your father pulled that particular little trick?' he shot at her in disgust. 'How do you suppose Randolph Gregory managed to put together his vast empire? A man who started with virtually nothing, and who's only a very mediocre businessman, with very little flair or imagination?'

'He's got where he is by sheer hard work,' Cassandra defended him. 'All right, so he's had a little luck along the way, but that's the way it goes.'

'The only "luck" he's had is what he's deliberately created! He leans on people, threatens to cut off vital contracts if they don't go along with him, uses the powerful financial connections he's built up to manoeuvre people into corners from which there's no escape—except the route that he offers them.'

'What you're saying is that he's a criminal,' Cassandra cried hotly. 'If you believe that, then you should take him to court! Let the law decide who's telling the truth.'

'Do you think I didn't try?' Jared growled. 'Only, to take someone to court, you have to have tangible proof. And your father always makes very sure there's never any of that. Skilful accounting, pressure on certain people so that they won't talk—he's had a lot of practice at that sort of thing. Even if you could begin to unravel all of it, my guess is that he's made absolutely certain that it won't lead directly back to him. A lot of people might eventually end up in gaol—but not your father.'

'Why should he?' she flashed back. 'As far as I'm concerned, he's done nothing wrong. The only person who says he has is you—and you're totally biased, because you lost out to him in a business deal.'

Jared seemed about to say something more. At the last moment, though, he gave a small shrug and turned away, as if he couldn't be bothered to argue about it any more.

'You're obviously not interested in the truth,' he said. 'But then, why should you be? You were born and raised a Gregory, and you've spent the last twenty-two years enjoying all the luxuries your father's wheelings and dealings could provide for you. You obviously don't want to do anything to put that at risk, and maybe lose your very comfortable life-style.'

'I work for a living,' Cassandra reminded him furiously. 'I'm not dependent on my father, and I certainly don't ask him to support me!'

'No?' Jared's eyebrows rose gently. 'Who provided the capital, when you started up your business?'

'Well—my father said I might as well borrow it from him as from the bank,' she said, a defensive note creeping into her voice. 'I don't see anything wrong with that,' she added staunchly.

'That rather depends. Did you pay him back?'

This time, a definite hint of colour crept into her face. 'I wanted to. But he refused to take it.'

'I see.' Somehow, that short comment from Jared made her feel about two inches high. It was a new sensation for her, and not one that she liked at all. 'How about your office?' he probed relentlessly. 'It's in a very fashionable part of London. The rent must be sky-high.'

She lifted her head defiantly. 'A friend of my father's owns the office block. He wasn't using those couple of rooms, so he let me have them at a reduced rent until he could find a permanent tenant.'

'And in eighteen months, he still hasn't found anyone who wants a small suite of offices in such a prime site? You really have been very fortunate, Miss Cassandra Gregory,' he mocked gently.

'Yes, I have,' she said stiffly. How dared this man insinuate that it had been anything else?

'One last thing,' Jared went on in a conversational tone. 'Your flat—did you buy it yourself?'

'It was a twenty-first birthday present,' Cassandra got out through gritted teeth.

'From your father?' It was a question that didn't need answering, and Cassandra stood there with her lips clenched tightly shut.

'All right, so my father paid for my flat. And maybe I *did* have a helping hand when I first set up my business. But I worked damned hard!' she defended herself fiercely. 'Most of what I achieved, I did on my own. And I won't let you—or anyone else—say that I didn't.'

'I'm not trying to run down what you've achieved,' replied Jared. 'I'm simply pointing out that it would have taken you far longer, and you would have had to work very much harder, if you hadn't been financed by Gregory money and had all the advantages of your father's business—and social—connections.'

That last gibe really hit home. For a long time, Cassandra had stubbornly closed her mind to the fact that a lot—in fact, most—of her early commissions had come from her father's friends and business acquaintances. She had told herself that she had earned them through her own right, that they hadn't come to her solely because she was her father's daughter. But now Jared Sinclair was making exactly that accusation, bringing all the old doubts flooding back into her mind again.

'I've had enough of this!' she muttered angrily. 'I'm going back to my room.'

'Not hungry any more?' he taunted her, catching

and holding her gaze until she felt the colour flare up in her face again. 'It's strange how the truth can so often take away your appetite.'

'It's got nothing to do with anything you've said,' she snapped back at him. 'It's just that it would choke me if I had to eat your food!'

And, with that, she whirled round and stalked out of the kitchen. She didn't go back to her bedroom, though. She knew it would only remind her of how she had been locked in last night, and she would get angry all over again. Instead, she headed for the drawing-room. As soon as she walked in, though, without any warning, memories of yesterday evening surged into her mind. All she could seem to think of was the way Jared had kissed her. No one had ever kissed her so impersonally. And yet her reaction had been far from impersonal. Even now, she could feel that odd weakness in her legs as she remembered exactly how those cool, firm lips had felt against hers.

'Damn!' she muttered to herself, in fierce irritation. 'Isn't there a room in this house that doesn't remind me of Jared Sinclair?'

In the end, she made her way to the main hall. Even with the sun shining, it was a cold, cheerless room. The stone-flagged floor still radiated a definite chill, the lack of furniture added to the general atmosphere of discomfort, and its only real asset was the view from the windows. As from the drawing-room, there was a magnificent panorama of glittering water and dappled mountain slopes. With the sun approaching its midday peak, the colours glowed even more brightly, forcing Cassandra to acknowledge the grandeur of the scene.

After a while, she found she could at last stop

thinking about Jared Sinclair. Instead, her thoughts began to wander back to her father. Although she would never have admitted it to Jared in a million years, she knew there were a lot of things about the relationship between herself and her father that bothered her—and had made her feel uneasy for quite some time. The main problem, she admitted with a frown, was his total possessiveness. He seemed unable to accept that she was an adult now, with her own life to lead, and a strong need to be completely independent. Rarely a day went by when he didn't either ring her, or perhaps even call by in person. He had fiercely disapproved of every boyfriend she had ever had—not that any of them had ever turned into serious relationships—and had seemed far happier when she was concentrating on her work, too busy to bother with men.

Cassandra gave a small sigh. She had to admit there were often times when she felt completely stifled. It was one reason why she had insisted on moving out of the family home when she was twenty-one. She still flinched when she remembered the awful rows there had been over that. For once, though, she had stood her ground, and in the end they had reached a compromise. He would let her go as long as he could buy the flat for her—and he had insisted that it had to be somewhere not too far away.

Sometimes—and rather guiltily—she thought his attitude was a little unnatural. On the other hand, there was a perfectly logical explanation for it. Her mother had died when Cassandra was very young, and since her father hadn't remarried, and had no close relatives, she supposed she was the only real family he had, the one constant factor in his life.

His little girl, who was always there, no matter what happened. Only, she wasn't a little girl any longer——

Her thoughts moved away from the problems of her personal relationship with her father, and fixed instead on the extraordinary accusations Jared had made against him. They had to be lies, of course, she told herself staunchly. Yet Jared had sounded so *certain*. And surely no one would go through with this incredible abduction unless he had a very good reason? Cassandra shook her head. The more she thought about it, the more confused she became. Just stick to basic facts, she ordered herself. Her father definitely wasn't a crook. This whole situation had come about because Jared Sinclair was obviously unstable.

Determined to stick to her own version of events, she marched out of the hall and back to the kitchen. To her relief, Jared was no longer there. Poking around in the cupboards, she found there was plenty of food, and she guessed Jared had been out earlier that morning to fetch in supplies. She cooked herself an enormous lunch and ate it, and when she went to wash up she found hot water gushing out of the tap.

'So he's found time to light the boiler,' she muttered to herself. 'How about the electricity?' She tried the light switch, and the single bulb suspended in the middle of the kitchen immediately lit up. 'He *has* had a busy morning. This place is practically civilised now.'

She decided it was a pity the same thing couldn't be said for Jared himself. Anyway, where was he? She didn't much like it when he was around, but for some reason she felt edgy when he was out of sight for too long.

A quick exploration of the ground floor revealed that he was in the drawing-room. As Cassandra peered round the door, she was a little astonished to find him sprawled out in the armchair, sound asleep.

In fact, he didn't look particularly well. There wasn't a lot of colour in his face, and there were definite dark smudges under his eyes. Cassandra remembered the coughing she had heard in the night, but easily pushed aside any stirrings of sympathy. She hoped he was coming down with a streaming cold! With luck, it would be a real stinker, sore throat, coughing and sneezing, a bright red 'nose—the lot!

Then something else occurred to her. If he was asleep, then he wouldn't hear if she left. All she had to do was to creep out, and—— She gave a grimace. And what? Walk umpteen miles in her totally impractical, high-heeled shoes? He would be awake and coming after her before she had gone any distance. Her eyes became thoughtful. What she really needed were the keys to his car. But where did he keep them?

Carefully, she looked all around the drawing-room. Then she gave a frustrated sigh. Obviously not in here. In his bedroom? It was possible, she supposed. It was far more likely that he kept them with him, though. That way, he could be certain she would never be able to get her hands on them.

She studied his sleeping figure thoughtfully. He was wearing jeans, a thick jumper, and a leather jacket. If he kept them in his jacket pocket, she might just be able to get them out. Providing she was careful, of course, and he wasn't a very light sleeper.

She knew it was risky, but what the hell? What did she have to lose?

Kicking off her high-heeled shoes that clicked so loudly on the floor, she tiptoed towards him. In a few seconds, she was right beside his chair, and he still hadn't stirred. Gingerly, she sank to her knees beside him. If the keys were in his jeans, she would never be able to fish them out without waking him. He would have to sleep like a log not to feel her probing fingers. But if they were in his jacket, she might just manage it.

Holding her breath, she let her fingers creep towards him; then she was actually touching the leather jacket. Please don't let my hands shake, she prayed. Inch by inch, her fingers crept inside, reaching down to the very bottom of his pocket. Then she caught her breath. She was sure she could feel something metallic——

A second later, Jared's hand slid up and smoothly locked itself around her wrist.

'My dear Miss Gregory, what*ever* are you looking for?' he murmured.

The blood hurtled into Cassandra's face and she tried to whip her hand away, but Jared's grip was too tight.

'I told you last night that I wasn't interested in you,' Jared mocked softly. 'I didn't realise that *I* was the one who was in danger of being seduced.'

'If you think that I——' she spluttered.

'What else can I think?' he said suavely. 'Not when I wake up and discover that you find me so irresistible that you can't keep your hands off me.'

'I was after your car keys!' she yelled at him. 'And you damned well know that!'

Jared gave an exaggerated sigh. 'How disappointing. I thought that we might be in for a very interesting afternoon.'

She shot a look of pure loathing at him. 'You are a snake! A slug! A worm!'

For the first time since they had met, a shadow of a genuine smile touched the hard corners of his mouth. 'And you're very different from the rather elegant and sophisticated girl who arrived here with me yesterday afternoon. More like a fishwife, in fact,' he said cheerfully. 'And I'm not so sure that it isn't an improvement. I always prefer it when people act naturally.'

'Then perhaps you'll enjoy this!' she got out through gritted teeth, and with her free hand she took a hefty swipe at him.

He stopped the clumsy blow easily, catching hold of her other wrist and not letting go. With both her wrists in his strong grip, she couldn't do much except squirm helplessly. After a while she went still again, realising it was quite useless to try and break free.

Jared's silver gaze looked down at her contemplatively. His face was only inches away, and this close it looked even more—disturbing, she thought with an unexpected shiver. It gave so little away, revealing nothing of his true feelings or his intentions.

'This is the sort of situation that gives rise to all sorts of possibilities,' he said musingly. 'A beautiful girl. And a man who's been celibate for rather longer than he intended——'

Alarm instantly flickered in Cassandra's eyes. She tried to hide it, but was sure he had seen it.

'Of course, I do realise what's expected of me in this sort of situation,' Jared went on in that same thoughtful tone. 'I should kiss that rather delectable mouth of yours. Perhaps bend my head a little further and explore those very perfect breasts. And who knows?' he continued, his gaze returning to hers and locking on to her eyes with almost hypnotic force. 'You may find you like it. Perhaps even want me to go further——'

No, she whispered. At least, that was what she meant to say. But, somehow, the word never came out, not even in a strangled mutter.

Jared smiled again, and this time it was the cold, unpleasant smile that she remembered so well. She had the awful feeling that he could see right inside her head and knew exactly what was going on there.

An instant later, he released her wrists. It was so unexpected that for several seconds she stayed exactly where she was, as if still locked in his hands.

'Sometimes, I wish I could be bothered with these games, that I could get some pleasure from them again. But I can't. Go away, Cassandra Gregory,' he said, his voice suddenly sounding very tired. 'You're gorgeous, but you're beginning to bore me.'

The insult wasn't deliberate, she was sure of that. He was simply speaking the truth. That didn't make it any easier to take, though. She wasn't used to being rejected out of hand, and she found herself deeply resenting it.

She was just about to flash back a scorching reply when she suddenly stopped herself. What on earth was she doing? She ought to be *grateful* this man wasn't interested in her, instead of instantly bristling at his dismissive attitude.

'If you find me that boring, why don't you just let me go?' she said rather curtly.

'Because I don't want to. Not yet. God knows, there are few enough pleasures left in my life. And one of them is looking at you, and knowing that right now Randolph Gregory is working himself up into a cold sweat, wondering where the hell you are, tormenting himself with the thought of what might have happened to you.'

'Sadist!' she hissed at him.

He didn't seem in the least disturbed by her accusation. Cassandra was beginning to wonder if there was anything that could touch this man; if there was any way of reaching him and making him see that what he was doing wasn't the act of a rational human being.

She decided to try a new tack. 'If your life's as meaningless as you say, then perhaps it's time you did something about it,' she challenged. 'I can't stand people who sit around moping and moaning, and won't do anything to help themselves.'

Jared's gaze flicked over her, bland and unemotional. 'My life is the way it is because of other people,' he said at last. 'There isn't anything I can do about that. And I can't change a single part of what has happened.'

'Can't? Or don't want to?' Cassandra accused scornfully. 'Perhaps it's easier to sit back and say, well, I've had a rough time, so that's a good excuse for opting out of things.'

'Perhaps it is,' he agreed offhandedly.

When he didn't say anything more, Cassandra stared at him in total exasperation. Trying to drag a genuine response out of this man was harder than running up Mount Everest on bare feet!

She turned away and was about to stalk out of the room, but at the last moment swung back and confronted him again.

'What exactly am I meant to *do* while I'm here?' she demanded. 'You might be perfectly content to laze around all day, just eating and sleeping, but I'm

bored! I'm used to working, to being occupied. I
don't like being idle.'

Jared shrugged. 'There are books, records—you
might find something you like. Or if you fancy
something more energetic, try going for a walk.'

'In these?' she said sarcastically, retrieving the
high-heeled shoes that she had earlier kicked off.

'It's not my fault if vanity made you dress entirely
inappropriately for this part of the country.'

'I thought I was coming to a civilised household,
where I'd be staying just long enough to decide if I
wanted to take on the job of planning the
redecoration and modernisation,' she reminded him
with a black scowl. 'I didn't know I was being hauled
off to the wilds by some savage, and kept here
against my will.'

'Life's full of little surprises, isn't it?' murmured
Jared. Then he rather pointedly closed his eyes, and
Cassandra got the hint. She was boring him again.
He wanted her to go.

Well, she was happy enough to comply. Being in
the same room as Jared Sinclair for more than a few
minutes was enough to give anyone high blood-
pressure!

The sun was still shining outside, and on impulse
she left the house and walked down the path. When
she reached the road, she looked wistfully in both
directions. If only a car would come whizzing by. She
could jump out in the road and stop it, and be away
from here before Jared had time to lever his idle
bones out of that chair.

Then she gave a grimace. There was virtually no
hope of that happening. This road led only to
Glenveil, and the unoccupied cottage a little further
along. The only people ever likely to come this way

were holiday-makers who had got completely lost, and there weren't many tourists in this part of the world this late in the year.

The impulse to get away from there was so strong, though, that she actually contemplated trying to walk to the nearest house, no matter how many miles away it might be. She even took a few steps, but almost at once the blisters on her feet began to rub painfully against her tight-fitting shoes.

'Drat!' she muttered. With dragging reluctance, she turned back to the house.

She had to admit that, like the loch and mountains, Glenveil looked better in the sunshine. The stonework was still dark, but at least it had lost its downright gloomy appearance. Cassandra ran a critical eye over it. If Jared would knock down that clutter of outbuildings, that would improve things even more. The house might look almost handsome.

Although she had slightly revised her opinion of it, she still didn't want to go back inside. It wasn't the house that was causing the faint ripple of goose-pimples over her skin, though. It was the thought of its owner. She didn't understand him and she couldn't get through to him. It was a new experience for her—usually, she could read male minds only too easily, and knew *exactly* what they were thinking. If she had some inkling of what was going on inside Jared's head, she might have felt less on edge.

All the same, she didn't have much choice. The sun was growing hazy as a faint mist began to gather over the mountains, and there was a definite chill in the air now. Wrapping her arms around herself, she very slowly retraced her steps up the path and then through the entrance to Glenveil.

Jared was no longer in the drawing-room, which

was a relief. She chucked a couple more logs on to the
fire, and then huddled over its warmth as the
temperature outside began to plummet. She could
feel the cold rising up from the stone-flagged floor,
with nothing except a couple of small, scattered rugs
to stop it. Cassandra grunted in annoyance. Hadn't
Jared Sinclair ever heard of carpets? He seemed
determined to live in as much physical discomfort as
possible.

She had to cook her own meal that evening,
because there was still no sign of Jared. Once or
twice, though, she could hear the faint sound of
coughing coming from upstairs, so she knew he was
still in the house. Perhaps his cold had got worse,
and he had taken himself off to bed. She didn't really
care enough to go up and find out. After she had
eaten, she found herself a book from the surprisingly
wide selection in one of the smaller side-rooms. Then
she curled up in the chair, in front of the fire, trying
to keep warm as she rather half-heartedly began to
read.

The house seemed very silent. Apart from the
occasional creaking of ancient woodwork, and the
spitting and crackling of the logs on the fire, there
wasn't a sound. After a while, it started to get on
Cassandra's nerves. Irritably, she flung her book
down and got to her feet.

'To hell with this!' she muttered. 'I might as well go
to bed.'

Like last night, her room felt freezing. She
undressed and scuttled into bed in record time, and
then curled up in a small ball, trying to get warm.

'An Eskimo would feel right at home here,' she
mumbled to herself. Then she closed her eyes very
tight, determined to get to sleep despite her frozen

hands and feet, and the deeper chill that lay somewhere inside of her.

Rather to her surprise, she succeeded. When she next opened her eyes, the room was still dark, but she had the feeling that she had been asleep for several hours. Then she wriggled rather uncomfortably. She needed to go to the bathroom. She was just about to get out of bed when she realised there was every possibility she was locked in, as she had been last night. Her face gathered into a furious frown. It would be the absolute end if she had to hammer on the door and yell for Jared to come and let her out!

When she tried the door, though, she was surprised to find it opened straight away. Had he forgotten to lock it? Or had he decided he could trust her? Cassandra's eyes gleamed. If he thought that, then he was in for one or two shocks over the next couple of days!

She hurried along to the bathroom, and on the way back realised she could hear the sound of a persistent fit of coughing echoing through the house. It seemed to be coming from behind a door that stood slightly ajar. For a few moments, she stood and looked at it. Should she go in? See if he was all right?

No, definitely not, she decided. Jared Sinclair didn't deserve any sympathy or attention. In fact, she hoped he felt thoroughly lousy.

She was just about to continue on her way back to her bedroom when another thought suddenly struck her. If he had felt so ill that he had forgotten to lock her door, perhaps this was something she could take advantage of.

Very alert now, she silently walked back to the door that was slightly open. Carefully, she pushed it a few more inches, so she could see right into the room.

A small lamp was still switched on, giving off enough light for her to see the bed fairly clearly. And what she saw made her heart suddenly leap.

Jared's eyes were open, but they gave the impression of being completely unfocused. And where his face had been very pale the previous afternoon, it was now touched with a high, unnatural colour.

Cassandra came further into the room, and then looked down at him with some satisfaction.

'Well, Mr Jared Sinclair,' she said softly. 'Somehow, I don't think you're much of a threat to me any more.'

The sound of her voice seemed to dimly register, because Jared turned his head towards her. It was odd to see those silver eyes so glazed. She was used to seeing them either cold and mocking, or deliberately unemotional. Now, they gave the impression of being strangely helpless, and for a moment something twisted a little painfully inside Cassandra. Then she lifted her shoulders and her gaze hardened. Oh, no, she wasn't going to let him get to her!

From the speed with which he had succumbed to this illness, she guessed it wasn't just a cold, but the 'flu. Probably one of the fairly virulent forty-eight-hour varieties. In a couple of days, he would be feeling weak, but fine again. But, by then, she wouldn't be around.

'Now, where have you put those car keys?' she said thoughtfully.

Jared was still staring at her, but he didn't seem to be making much sense of what she was saying. He muttered something in a hoarse voice, but it was just a slurred mumble and Cassandra ignored it.

She glanced around, and saw his clothes lying in an untidy heap on the floor. He had obviously felt too bad to do anything except drag them off and crawl into bed.

'Do you still keep your car keys in your pocket, Mr Sinclair?' asked Cassandra with a bright smile, almost beginning to enjoy herself. As she reached for the leather jacket, something appeared to click inside Jared's head and he made an attempt to sit up. The effort was obviously too much for him, though. With a fierce growl, he fell back on the bed again, his skin glistening with sweat, and his breathing coming in short, alarmingly wheezy gasps.

Cassandra slid her hand into the pocket of the jacket, and her smile broadened as her fingers closed around a small bunch of keys.

'Very careless of you,' she taunted him, 'leaving them where I could so easily find them. But also very convenient.' She moved a little closer to the bed and dangled them just in front of him. 'Do you know what this means? That your clever little plan has fallen apart. Such a shame,' she mocked. 'It was all so carefully thought out, and you were enjoying it so much. Now it's ruined, and all because you caught the 'flu. Still, you know what they say about the best laid plans of mice and men——'

A flicker of comprehension briefly showed again in Jared's eyes, and one hand came up, as if to grab her wrist and wrench away the keys. Cassandra easily dodged away, though.

'I'm afraid that won't work, not this time,' she informed him with some satisfaction. 'In fact, it seems to me that you don't have a great deal going for you at the moment. And that's good, because it means that I don't even have to hurry. I can go back to my room, get dressed and packed in my own good time, and then just walk away from this hellhole of a place. No, not walk away—*drive* away,' she corrected herself, staring down at him triumphantly. 'In your car!'

Jared began to say something, but was then seized with a fit of coughing that obviously left him quite exhausted. Cassandra firmly squashed a quick surge of pity.

'Do you expect me to feel sorry for you?' she asked, forcing her voice to remain hard. 'Well, I'm afraid that's asking too much. As far as I'm concerned, you can go to hell, Mr Jared Sinclair. And if we ever set eyes on each other again, it'll be in a court of law, because I intend to make sure that you go to gaol for what you've done to me these last couple of days!'

Keeping her eyes deliberately averted from the man on the bed, she turned and marched out of the room. A quarter of an hour later, she was dressed, packed, and ready to leave. The car started first time, but, as she swung it away from the house, she reluctantly stopped for a few moments and stared up at the one lighted window in the darkened house of Glenveil.

Her conscience suddenly gave a strong twinge, but she deliberately ignored it.

'I *won't* feel any sympathy for him,' she told herself fiercely. 'And I definitely won't feel guilty about leaving him.'

With fresh determination, she headed the car towards the road and drove off into the night.

CHAPTER FOUR

IT WAS full daylight by the time she finally reached Inverness airport. She dumped Jared's car in a no-parking area, and hoped the police came and towed it away. As far as she was concerned, the more trouble she could cause for him, the better! Then she caught an early flight to London, and was back in her own flat by late morning.

It felt odd to be back home again. Everything seemed so—well, so normal, she said to herself rather ruefully. When something traumatic happened to you, somehow you expected the whole world to fall apart in sympathy. Everyone was going about their everyday lives, though, quite oblivious to the fact that a stranger had walked in and just snatched her away from everything for a couple of days.

For some reason, she began to feel strangely weak as soon as she was safely back home. Ridiculous, she lectured herself, a little impatiently. The danger was past now; she could relax, and get on with her life again. Yet she had the feeling that, from now on, she would never be able to feel completely relaxed. She would always be haunted by the knowledge that Jared Sinclair was out there somewhere, perhaps planning further revenge on her for whatever he imagined her father had once done to him.

Cassandra shivered. It wasn't a pleasant feeling, knowing you were that vulnerable. And Jared was so unreasonable, so obsessed with his hatred for her

father. You couldn't talk to him, convince him that no
sane man would continue indefinitely with this
vendetta against the Gregory family.

Yet when she remembered his cool silver eyes, the
logical reasons he had given for his behaviour, it was
equally hard to convince herself that he was actually
crazy. Another picture flashed through her
mind—she saw him lying on that bed, sweating and
weak, all alone in that cold, empty house. He could
develop pneumonia, become very seriously ill,
even——

Stop it! she ordered herself sharply. There was no
need to get melodramatic over it. He had 'flu, that
was all. He looked like a strong man—he would soon
get over it. And if he was alone, that was entirely his
fault. If he lived like an ordinary human being instead
of shutting himself away in that freezing barn of a
place in the middle of nowhere, he wouldn't be
facing those problems. Whatever happened to him
was entirely his own fault—and no more than he
deserved!

The ringing of the telephone interrupted her rather
disjointed and confused thoughts. With a hand that
wasn't quite steady, she reached for the receiver.

Before she had time to say a word, she heard her
father's voice. 'Cassie?'

He was the only one who shortened her name, and
ever since her teens she had hated it. It
was—childish, she told herself. 'Cassie' sounded like
a little girl's name. She had asked him over and over
to use her full name, but he only smiled and said,
'You'll always be my sweet little Cassie, no matter
how old you are.'

And now, for some reason, it was irritating her
all over again. Why was she worrying about it at

a time like this? she wondered with a wry shake of her head. She had far more important things that ought to be occupying her!

'Cassie, where the hell have you been?' asked her father anxiously. 'I've been phoning you over and over these last couple of days, but I couldn't get any reply. No one knew where you were, not even your secretary. Why didn't you leave a message, or give me a ring to let me know where you'd be?'

Cassandra knew that she ought to be blurting out the whole story, and demanding that he do something about the outrageous thing that had happened to her. Instead, she found herself unaccountably annoyed by her father's attitude. All right, this time he had every right to be worried. After all, she *had* been virtually abducted, and it was only by sheer luck that she had got away. But what if she had just decided to go off with a friend for a couple of days? Perhaps even a male friend? Didn't she have any right to a private life—even a sex life, if that was what she wanted? Did she really have to account to her father for the way she spent every minute of her days—and nights?

'It's—a rather long story,' she said at last, still slightly amazed that she hadn't come straight out and told him what had happened to her. 'And rather a complicated one. Can I come round and see you? It's difficult to talk about it over the phone.'

'Come round straight away,' he said without hesitation. 'I'll be waiting for you.'

Cassandra put down the phone, and then wondered why she had the strong feeling that she ought to deal with this herself; that it was time she stopped automatically running to her father with all her problems. Sometimes, she felt as if the past few

years had been a long—and mainly unsuccessful
—struggle to break away from him. He seemed
determined not to let her grow up, though, and he
knew so many subtle ways of keeping her dependent
on him. The trouble was, she had almost got to the
point where she was tired of fighting him. It was so
much easier just to give in, and let him take charge of
all the things that troubled or bothered her.

Her mouth curled into a dry smile. Most people
who knew her wouldn't believe she had this
problem. They saw her as independent, strong-
minded, even sophisticated. And so she was, up to a
point. But when she went anywhere near her father,
the whole façade just fell apart, and she knew the
only real freedom she had was what he allowed her.
She sighed softly. It was something that an outsider
would find so hard to understand. They wouldn't
know how he had dominated her childhood, a
charismatic man who had spoiled her shamelessly,
but demanded to share her life, allowing her no close
friendships with anyone else. And they certainly
wouldn't know how hard she had found it to return
that smothering love. That was her own guilty and
closely guarded secret.

And he still hadn't released his grip on her, even
thought she was now a fully grown adult.
Sometimes, she thought she would go right through
her life still being his 'little girl'—and the prospect
secretly appalled her.

Yet here she was, running back to Daddy again.
Any time she was in trouble, she trotted straight
round to him. Old habits were hard to break, and
over the years he had found so many ways of making
sure that she kept to a certain pattern of behaviour.

Half an hour later, she was knocking on his office

door. It opened at once, and her father stood there with a light frown on his face.

'Come on in. Are you all right? Where have you *been*?'

The instant barrage of questions—and his automatic assumption that he had the right to know where she had spent the last couple of days—aroused her old sense of resentment all over again. She had been about to blurt out the entire story, to demand that her father find Jared Sinclair and make him pay for what he had done to her. Instead, though —amazing even herself—she walked into her father's office and sat down in the chair in front of his desk.

'Before we get round to that, I'd like to know one or two things,' she told him in a voice that sounded almost as cool as Jared's had been.

Her father came over and sat opposite her. 'About what?' he demanded. 'Cassie, what's this all about?' His gaze swept over her suspiciously. 'You look—different,' he muttered at last. 'Older, somehow, not quite like my Cassie.' His face darkened. 'My God, is it some man? Is that where you've been these last couple of days?'

'A man's certainly involved,' she agreed. Then, as his features became positively thunderous, she added, 'But not in the sense that you mean. Either way, it isn't important——'

'Not important?' her father cut in incredulously. 'How can you sit there and say that?'

'Quite easily,' she replied, still astonishing herself with her own calmness. It was as if she had been through so much the last couple of days that she had run clean out of emotional responses. 'I'm twenty-two years old. I think that's quite old enough to run my private life as I please.' Her voice a little crisper now, she went on, 'But that isn't what I want to talk about right now. I want you to tell me about Glenveil Toys.'

When she had first walked into his office, she had never had any intention of asking him such a question. In fact, nothing about this conversation was turning out the way she had expected. With some detachment, she wondered if she was suffering from some kind of delayed shock. She certainly felt almost light-headed. Yet, at the same time, her mind was perfectly clear.

She studied her father as if he were a stranger. His face was very familiar, but today she was seeing things that she couldn't remember ever noticing before. He had said that she looked different, and yet so did he. She realised that his good looks were beginning to become rather florid, so that he was no longer the handsome man she remembered from her childhood, dazzling her with his appearance. And he was putting on weight. Too many business lunches, she thought dispassionately. But it was his eyes which kept drawing her attention. Had they always had that hooded, guarded look, as if he were a man who had a great many secrets he needed to keep hidden? And why hadn't she noticed before that they had no real depth, no warmth? Jared Sinclair's eyes had often been cold, and yet they had never aroused in her this faint sense of repellence that she was experiencing now.

'Glenveil Toys,' she repeated firmly. 'I want to know all about it.'

'Why this sudden interest in a second-rate little company?' demanded her father.

She was instantly alert. 'It wasn't second-rate when you bought it, was it?'

'No, it wasn't,' he said irritably. 'How was I to know it was virtually a one-man show? These last few months, it's gone steadily downhill. No new lines worth talking about, and I can't find anyone who can design a new range of toys to take over from the old products.'

'What do you mean, it was a one-man show?' Cassandra was sure she knew exactly what he meant, but for some reason she needed to hear her father say it.

'I'm talking about Sinclair, the previous owner,' he muttered angrily. 'He designed every new toy they produced. It turns out no one else can touch him. We've brought out a few new products since then, but they've all been mediocre and sales are dropping away faster and faster.' He scowled. 'After I'd taken over the company, I told Sinclair he could stay on, offered him a damn good salary and generous perks. He didn't even have the decency to reply to my offer. Just vanished into the blue, and no one's heard of him since.'

Not until a couple of days ago, Cassandra told herself silently. When he walked into my life, and turned it upside-down.

She looked at her father again. 'I've heard one or two rumours,' she said carefully. 'People have said that the way you took over his company wasn't—well, entirely fair.'

'Nothing's particularly fair in business,' growled her father. 'You don't get anywhere unless you push a little, take advantage of circumstances.'

A faint feeling of nausea was beginning to gather in the pit of Cassandra's stomach. She had never heard her father talk like this before—perhaps because she had never bothered to question him about his business life, or the way he conducted his affairs. Jared was right, she realised with another wave of unpleasant sickness. She had taken her father's money, enjoyed a very comfortable life-style, and never once questioned where that wealth had come from or how it had been acquired. Wasn't there something extremely immoral about that?

'You still haven't told me exactly how you acquired Glenveil Toys,' she reminded him, her voice not totally steady now.

Her father shrugged. 'You'd be bored by all the complicated details. Let's just say that I realised it was an advantageous time to step in. Sinclair's mind wasn't on the business—I suppose that was only to be expected after the accident—and he didn't even notice that I'd whipped the whole thing out from under him until it was too late for him to do anything about it.'

Her father sat back in his chair and grinned with satisfaction, as if the memory gave him great pleasure. And there was an expectant look on his face, as if he were waiting for her to applaud his business acumen. Cassandra's mind had latched on to just one phrase, though, and her head came up sharply.

'Accident? What accident?'

'His wife and kid were killed. A drunken driver mounted the pavement and mowed them down.' Her father shrugged. 'Tragic I suppose,' he said, not sounding in the least bit sorry. 'But a bit of luck for me. Sinclair let things slip for a while after that, and that gave me the chance I'd been looking for. By the end of the year, Glenveil Toys belonged to *me*.' Then he looked rather peeved again. 'Only it didn't turn out to be the sound investment I'd expected. Without

Sinclair, the company just began to slide. I might have to dump it before too long—that's if I can find anyone fool enough to buy it.'

Cassandra wasn't even listening any more. Her heart felt as if it had actually stopped beating. My God, Jared had lost both his wife and child in one horrific accident? No wonder he had lost virtually all interest in the business of living, and found so little pleasure in anything!

Then the rest of it slowly began to sink in. Her father had *deliberately* taken advantage of the tragedy. Knowing that no man could concentrate fully on his business affairs after such a devastating event, her father had chosen that time to step in and take Jared's company away from him. Whether he had done it fairly, or used totally unscrupulous methods, no longer seemed important. The very fact that he had done it at all was suddenly more than she could stomach.

Without even realising she was moving, she slowly got out of her chair and began to walk towards the door.

Her father glanced at her sharply. 'Where are you going?'

'I don't know,' she muttered, in a voice that didn't sound in the least like her own.

'Cassie, come back!' he ordered. 'There's a lot we've still got to talk about.'

'There's nothing more I want to say to you right now,' she replied in a low tone.

In fact, right at this moment she felt as if she never wanted to talk to him again. She seemed to be seeing him clearly for the first time in her life, looking at him with the unbiased eyes of a adult instead of as a dutifully loving child. A part of her had always been

aware that he could be a hard man. And she had
known that he was ruthlessly competitive, that he
couldn't bear to lose. But—perhaps deliberately—she
had closed her eyes to a lot of his less pleasant
qualities. She couldn't do that any longer, though.
He had virtually thrown them in her face, *proud* of the
way he had taken over Glenveil Toys, taking
advantage of the tragedy that had hit another man's
life.

He was still saying something to her as she walked
out, but she wasn't listening. All she could hear was
a small voice echoing inside her head. His wife and
child . . . His wife and child . . . Cassandra
shuddered. What on earth must it be like to go
through a hell like that?

She went directly back to her flat, and then just sat
there for most of the afternoon, staring blankly at the
wall. She couldn't seem to think; too much had
happened over the last couple of days, and it was all
mixed up inside her head in a tangled mess. As
evening draw in, she automatically cooked a meal
and ate it, without tasting a single thing. And when
she finally went to bed, she closed her eyes, but
didn't sleep.

Early next morning, she got out of bed with a new
sense of purpose. During the long night, quite a few
things seemed to have fallen into place, and she
knew what she had to do. It didn't take her long to
pack a bag. Then she reached for the phone and
dialled the number of her part-time secretary.

'Susan?' she said, when a rather sleepy voice
answered at the other end. 'This is Cassandra. I'm
going to be away for a while—no, I don't know quite
how long. Can you take care of things at the office? If
anything urgent comes up, deal with it as you think

best. And if any new clients get in touch, try and stall them. I'll contact them when I get back. No, I'm afraid you can't ring me. Where I'm going, there isn't any phone.'

Since Susan was a competent, level-headed girl, Cassandra was confident she could deal with the day-to-day routine while she was away. If anything else came up—too bad. It would just have to wait.

Just minutes after she had replaced the receiver, the phone rang. Cassandra instinctively knew it was her father. For just an instant, her hand reached out automatically to answer it, then she realised what she was doing, and stopped, her mouth setting into a hard line. His 'little Cassie' wasn't at his beck and call any longer. Let him ring as often as he liked. He wouldn't be getting an answer.

A couple of hours later, she was on a flight to Scotland. Was she behaving sensibly? she asked herself more than once. Even rationally? Probably not, she conceded. But she didn't feel that she had any choice. She had walked out on a sick man, which was a pretty lousy thing to do, and for her own peace of mind she had to make sure he was all right. OK, so Jared's own behaviour had been pretty bizarre, not to mention illegal. Rather late in the day, though, she was forced to admit there had been extenuating circumstances. And, despite all the harsh words he had thrown at her, she was certain it had never been his intention to actually harm her in any way.

After her plane landed at Inverness, she found Jared's car was still at the airport. Someone had simply moved it to a legal parking space. She paid the parking fee, and minutes later was behind the wheel, driving rather too quickly along the narrow roads that wound between rolling hills and higher ridges of mountain. She didn't notice the russet glow that had begun to touch the Highlands, the sparkling streams, or the wider waters of the lochs. Even a solitary eagle soaring high overhead didn't distract her attention. All she seemed to be seeing were pictures inside her head, of a man who had looked extremely ill when she had walked away from him without even a backward glance.

What state would he be in now? Surely he would be feeling better by this time? she argued with herself a little frantically. Perhaps he would even be up—and if he were, how he would laugh at the way she had come rushing up here, with all sorts of wild fears flashing through her mind!

Only, Jared Sinclair didn't laugh, she reminded herself with new grimness. Nor was that very surprising, considering what he had been through during the past few months.

She pressed her foot down even harder on the accelerator, and was glad the roads were clear. Her driving was erratic, to say the least, as if reflecting her state of mind.

Then Glenveil finally came into view. The afternoon was bright and sunny, showing the house off to its best advantage. With the backdrop of tall pines and impressive mountains, Glenveil seemed to have taken on a new grandeur and dignity. 'Romantic' was how Jared had once described it, and today it fully lived up to that description. Cassandra half expected to see a kilted piper on the turret, or the ghost of some old laird flitting through the shadows. Nothing stirred, though. The house seemed totally deserted, as if no one had lived there for years.

Cassandra brought the car to a skidding halt, cut the engine, and then hurried to the front entrance.

She didn't have a key, but it didn't matter. The door wasn't locked. She turned the handle and pushed it open, then stepped more slowly inside.

The silence was almost oppressive. She called out once, rather falteringly, then jumped slightly as her voice echoed rather eerily back to her. No one answered her call and her heart began to thump rather faster.

Although, quite suddenly, it was the last thing she wanted to do, she slowly began to climb the stairs. Goose-pimples covered her skin now, and they weren't caused entirely by the familiar chill inside the house. What she was afraid of more than anything was what she was going to find when she reached the top of the stairs, and opened the door to Jared's bedroom.

Would the room be empty? Or would he still be there? And if he was, would he be——?

She closed her mind to the terrifying possibilities that immediately rushed into her head. Instead, she steadily walked on, across the landing on the first floor to a door that still stood ajar. Just as she had left it when she had rushed out, the night before last——

It took every scrap of nerve she had to inch it open a little further, allowing her to see right into the room. And when she finally found the courage to look inside, she instantly caught her breath and gave a small groan.

There was the bed, with the sheets and blankets heaped in total disarray. And in the middle of the chaos lay a male body, frighteningly still, arms and legs flung out in a haphazard fashion.

'Oh, God, no!' Cassandra moaned.

At that, Jared moved his head, coughed a couple of times, and then opened his eyes and looked at her.

'You're not dead,' she breathed in utter relief.

'Apparently not,' he agreed, his voice sounding hoarse but quite lucid. 'I might *feel* like it, but it doesn't seem to have actually happened.'

Cassandra ran her fingers shakily through her hair. 'Damn it, you gave me a fright!' Then, realising he was probably expecting some kind of explanation for her presence here, she added a little awkwardly, 'I've come back.'

Jared's silver gaze regarded her steadily. 'I didn't know you'd been away.'

She stared at him. 'But—didn't you miss me? You *must* have done.'

His dark brows drew together a fraction. 'What day is it?'

'Thursday.'

'Then Wednesday seems to have gone missing. I can't remember anything since Tuesday afternoon.'

He coughed again, and Cassandra looked around with some concern.

'This room is like a fridge. If I don't get some heat going in here, you'll end up with pneumonia.'

'I've already had it,' he said calmly.

Her eyes opened wide. 'You have? When?'

'A few months ago. I eventually got over it, but it's left a few irritating side-effects. Whenever I get a cold or the 'flu, I end up like this, completely knocked out for a couple of days.'

He said it so matter-of-factly that Cassandra wanted to hit him. What was wrong with the man? Didn't he *care* what happened to him? Then she bit back her angry retort. He had already answered that question himself. No, he didn't care. Everything he said, everything he did, made that perfectly clear.

'If you've been in that bed since Tuesday, then the sheets must need changing,' she said in a more practical tone of voice.

His eyes briefly gleamed with a familiar mocking

light. 'I think I must have left it a couple of times—for basic necessities.'

'In that case, you should be able to get out of it now,' she said firmly. 'I can't remake it with you still in it.'

It clearly took some effort, but Jared finally managed to sit up and swing his legs over the side. A fit of coughing made him pause for a moment, and Cassandra was very glad of that. She hadn't realised until this moment that he was totally naked!

'I'll—er—go and find some clean sheets,' she muttered, and hurriedly left the room.

Outside on the landing, she was annoyed to find her face was flaming. How childish! she lectured herself furiously. Anyone would think she was completely unfamiliar with the male anatomy!

Finding the sheets took longer than she had expected. Eventually, she found a heap of them tucked away in a cupboard in one of the bathrooms. By the time she eventually returned to Jared's room, her face was back to its normal colour again, and she kept telling herself that she felt perfectly calm and in control of things.

All the same, she shot a quick, furtive glance in Jared's direction as she went into the room. Then she let out a silent sigh of relief. He was wearing a bathrobe now, and sitting in a chair by the side of the bed.

He still didn't look at all well, but he was obviously very aware of what was going on. The fever had passed, leaving him weak but quite clear-headed again.

It didn't take her long to strip the bed. Then she began to unfold the fresh sheets and tuck them into place.

'I couldn't find any pyjamas,' she said, as she shook out the quilt and smoothed it over the remade bed.

'That's not very surprising,' remarked Jared. 'I never wear any.'

Cassandra felt herself flushing all over again. Thoroughly irritated with herself, she straightened up and said rather acidly, 'Then it's hardly surprising you're coughing and wheezing. This house has got to be one of the coldest places on earth. Anyone who sleeps here naked—and in an unheated room—deserves absolutely everything that he gets.'

'You're such a sympathetic girl,' Jared mocked lightly.

She instantly felt ashamed. He had been through enough. He didn't need to be spoken to with such sharpness.

Almost as if reading her mind, Jared added immediately, 'I don't mind. I'm sick of sympathy. You can only cope with so much, and then you start to feel as if you're drowning in it.' He hauled himself to his feet. It seemed to take the last of his strength, but Cassandra knew better than to offer a steadying hand.

He shot her an exhausted, but faintly taunting smile. 'Unless you want to be offended all over again, you'd better turn your back. I'm about to take off this robe and get back into bed.'

'I wasn't offended,' Cassandra denied at once, furious that he had noticed her confused reaction to his nakedness. 'I was just——' Her voice trailed away. She wasn't at all sure how to describe the feelings that had swept over her.

'Just what? Impressed?' Jared suggested, his eyes glinting as he shook off the bathrobe and tumbled tiredly into bed. 'That would definitely give my male ego a boost. And it feels as if it could do with it, at the moment——'

Cassandra glared at him indignantly, but then found he had fallen asleep the moment he had finished speaking. Her expression changed, and she let out a small sigh. Coming back here had been every bit as difficult as she had thought it would be. She might feel desperately sorry for Jared, but that still didn't stop her from responding to his subtle gibes with a hot flare of temper. Not that it really mattered, she excused herself. He had made it perfectly clear that he didn't want her sympathy, that he had already had a surfeit of other people's pity.

What he needed right now was purely practical help, she decided. That was the way she could be most useful. She set about clearing the cold ashes from the grate, and then relaid the fire. It was a fairly inexpert job, but she finally managed to get it to light, and felt a deep sense of satisfaction as she saw the flames beginning to build steadily, throwing out a warm glow.

There wasn't much she could do after that. Jared was still soundly asleep, and she didn't think he would appreciate it if she woke him up to ask if he wanted a hot drink, or something to eat. With a last long look at him—just to make sure he was all right, she told herself firmly—she tiptoed out of the room, leaving the door half-open so she would hear him if he called out.

She took her bag up to the room she had slept in before, and slowly unpacked. It felt odd to be back again. She hadn't expected to set foot in this house a second time—and certainly not voluntarily. After her clothes were stowed away in the cavernous wardrobe, she made her way downstairs to the kitchen. Jared might not want anything to eat yet, but she was starving.

Dusk was setting in now, and she clicked down the light switch. Nothing happened, though. Cassandra muttered something very rude under her breath. The generator had obviously stopped, and she had no idea how to get it going again. That meant cooking and eating by candlelight—very romantic, but she would have preferred a bright electric glow!

Once her meal was finished and cleared away, she realised she felt very tired. She had had virtually no sleep last night, and she was just about dead on her feet.

She blew out most of the candles, leaving just one to light her way upstairs. Fixing it into a holder, she then made her way up to the first floor, shutting her mind to the fact that Glenveil looked distinctly spooky at night, especially with the candlelight sending shadows jumping and dancing ahead of her.

Her newfound conscience reminded her that she ought to check on Jared before she crawled into bed. She poked her head round his door, but the candle didn't give off enough light for her to see him clearly. She had to go right inside and stand over his bed in order to see if he was still asleep.

He was. The room felt much warmer now, and she put a few more logs on the fire to keep it going, before returning for one last look at Jared. A little anxiously, she peered at his skin. Was it slightly damp with sweat, or was it just the flickering candlelight creating an optical illusion?

Rather tentatively, she reached out and laid her palm against his shoulder. To her relief, his skin felt cool and dry. Then the sound of his voice made her nearly die of shock.

'Really, Cassandra,' he murmured reprovingly, without even opening his eyes. 'Every time I wake up, I find you haven't been able to resist the urge to touch me.'

'I was checking to see if you were still running a temperature,' she said furiously, hurriedly snatching her hand away.

'Mmm. That doesn't sound like a very plausible

excuse to me.' Before she could say anything, his eyes finally opened and fixed on her, making her feel distinctly edgy. 'What on earth are you playing at?' he enquired, his voice sounding almost amused as his gaze finally switched to the candle she was holding. 'The lady of the lamp?'

She wished she could hold the candle perfectly still. Its wavering light was giving away the fact that she couldn't quite keep her fingers steady.

'It may have escaped your attention, but the generator isn't working,' she told him stiffly. 'Anyway, since you're obviously all right, I'm going to bed,' she added.

'Sure you don't want to climb in with me?' Jared teased gently. 'Isn't that the time-honoured way of keeping an invalid warm? And you do keep telling me how very cold it is in this house.'

'I think you must still be feverish,' Cassandra retorted sharply. 'Otherwise, you wouldn't be gabbling all this nonsense.'

'It's entirely possible,' he agreed, without rancour. 'Then how about another traditional remedy? The cool hand against the hot brow? I rather like the touch of your skin,' he mused, to her astonishment—and fast-growing sense of unease. 'Very smooth, very fine. One day, it's going to give some man a great deal of pleasure.'

'That is *enough*,' she got out in a strangled voice. 'Else you'll be getting the cold water treatment instead of a cool hand!'

'I don't think you should speak like that to an invalid,' Jared reminded her. 'We're meant to be pampered and cosseted. Given everything we need,' he went on meaningfully, with a brief but bright flicker of his eyes.

Cassandra stared apprehensively back into the silver gaze. Something burned hotly in the depths— something she had never seen before.

He had obviously started to run a temperature again, she told herself firmly. It often happened at night, the recurrence of a fever. Then she jumped violently. Jared's finger had lightly stroked the back of her wrist.

'Somehow, I don't think you're going to take up my offer to share my bed,' he said a little regretfully. 'Even on purely medicinal grounds,' he added, with a rather strange smile.

'You're right,' she snapped. 'I'm not.'

'Sure?'

'Absolutely certain!'

'Then I may as well go back to sleep.' And to her astonishment—and unexpected sense of pique—he did precisely that.

Cassandra backed away from the bed, but then paused in the doorway for a couple of minutes. For some odd reason, she seemed to be finding it very hard to leave the room. Finally, she turned away and walked slowly to her own room on legs that didn't feel very steady.

'You were tired, and he was half-delirious again,' she told herself over and over, as if trying very hard to convince herself that was the truth of it. 'That's the only reason you had that extraordinary conversation.'

And she *was* tired. Absolutely bone-weary. Yet, when she climbed into her own cold bed and pulled the thick quilt closer around her, trying to get warm, for the second night running she found it impossible to sleep. Worse than that, she couldn't seem to shut up a little voice inside her head, which kept telling her how much more snug and comfortable she would feel if she were sharing a bed with Jared Sinclair.

CHAPTER FIVE

IN THE morning, Cassandra found she didn't want to open Jared's bedroom door and have to face him again. She didn't even know what she was doing here. She kept telling herself that she must have been out of her mind to come back to Glenveil again. Either that, or she was turning into some kind of masochist!

Still arguing furiously with herself, trying to convince herself that, if she had a single ounce of sense, she would simply pack her things and head straight back to London, she reluctantly pushed open his door. Then she blinked hard. His bed was empty! Where was he? Her gaze skipped anxiously round the room. Then she let out a sigh of relief as she saw Jared was sitting in the chair by the window.

'You're out of bed,' she said, slightly unnecessarily.

'It rather looks like it,' Jared concurred.

'You're feeling better?'

'That depends on how you look at it. My head certainly feels a lot clearer this morning. On the other hand, if I move too quickly, the entire room does several somersaults. And if I try to stand up again, I've a nasty feeling I'll fall flat on my face.'

He still looked a very unhealthy colour, but his eyes were bright and clear. And right now they were regarding her rather thoughtfully.

Cassandra nervously cleared her throat. 'I suppose you don't—er—don't remember very much of the past couple of days. I mean, you *were* delirious a lot of the time,' she went on guardedly.

'There do seem to be quite a few blank spots inside my head,' agreed Jared.

'Even last night, you really didn't seem to know what was going on.' She hadn't meant it to sound like a question, and was annoyed that she seemed to have so little control over her own voice when this man was around.

'Didn't I?' Her nerve-ends gently quivered as his tone turned suddenly and unexpectedly velvety. 'If you say so, then that's how it must have been,' he continued smoothly.

Cassandra wished she had the courage to come straight out and ask him if he had been raving with a fever last night, or if he had known perfectly well what he had been saying. Normally, she wasn't a coward. Only one other man had ever had the power to reduce her to this sort of ineffectual helplessness, and that was her father.

She lifted her head. She didn't want to think about him this morning. Instead, she took a firmer grip on herself and stepped further into the room.

'Since you're up, I may as well make the bed,' she said briskly. 'From the look of it, you had a rather restless night.'

Jared's silver eyes gleamed briefly. 'I believe that I did. Not that I *remember* much of it, of course,' he finished silkily.

Cassandra's own eyes suddenly blazed ominously. She had had enough of this. She was in no mood for any of his sly mockery this morning. She was tired, she felt edgy, and, worst of all, she knew she just didn't know how to cope with this man.

'That's it, I've had enough!' she flung at him

irritably. 'You can make your own bed, get your own meals, clear out that grate and light that fire yourself! I've just gone off-duty.'

Jared didn't seem in the least perturbed. She had forgotten how impossible it was to rile this man.

'The question is,' he said, in an interested voice, 'whatever made you come back in the first place? If I'd been you, I'd have got the hell out of here and never come within a hundred miles of the place again.'

'You're right,' she retorted. 'That's exactly what I should have done.'

'So—why didn't you?'

Cassandra wasn't sure that she wanted to answer that question. And particularly not now, when her entire nervous system seemed to be teetering on the edge of a minor collapse.

'You were ill—and on your own,' she muttered at last. 'I didn't know if you had any friends or family you could contact, who'd come and look after you.' She raised her head and looked at him. 'Was there anyone?'

'Probably not. I've lost touch with most of my friends this last year. As for my family—my parents are both dead, and I don't have any brothers or sisters.'

'Then it's as well that I did come. In fact, you ought to be grateful that someone showed a bit of concern for you.'

Jared merely looked sceptical. 'I kept you here against your will, and didn't exactly treat you well,' he reminded her. 'Under those sort of circumstances, no one in their right mind would give a damn about my welfare. Yet you came back.'

'Anyone would have done the same. It's a simple

question of—of humanity,' she finished rather weakly.

His gaze thoughtfully drifted over her. 'Oh, I don't think that there's anything *simple* about you, Cassandra,' he said softly. 'If you came back, then it was because you had your own very good reasons.'

She wished he would stop looking at her. She kept getting the impression that he could see right inside her head, and she resented that. She was here to get on with the practical tasks necessary to help him get over his illness, and that was all. Once he was on his feet again, she could leave with a clear conscience. And in the meantime, he had no right—no right at all!—to question her motives, or to pry into her private thoughts.

Forgetting that, just a few minutes earlier, she had threatened to walk out without lifting a single finger to help him, she hurried over to the bed and began to straighten the sheets. The best thing, she told herself, would be to ignore him completely. Get on with what she had to do, and then get out of here.

It was so much harder than she had thought, though. Even though she refused to look at him, she knew that silver gaze was resting on her as she moved about the room. Not that he was really interested in her, she silently assured herself. He was just watching her because there was nothing else to do. Invalids did that; it helped to break the boredom of their day.

Yet it was hard—if not downright impossible!—to think of Jared as an invalid. He might be as weak as a kitten right now—he might even fall over if he tried to get up and walk around—but he still didn't give the impression of being in the least helpless. Even just sitting there, not moving a muscle, he seemed to radiate an odd sort of danger signal which her raw nerves only too easily picked up. What kind of danger? she wondered warily. She didn't know—and she didn't intend to find out!

With the bed finally remade and the fire beginning to blaze brightly again, Cassandra reluctantly turned to face Jared.

'Do you want some breakfast?'

'Just something to drink. And I think I'd like to go back to bed.'

She shrugged. 'There's nothing to stop you.'

'I'm afraid that there is. I don't think I can make it unless you lend me a shoulder to lean on.'

Instantly, she stiffened. 'You made it from the bed to that chair without any help,' she pointed out.

'Yes, I did. But not for the first time, I over-estimated what I was capable of. It was definitely a one-way trip. I got this far—but I can't get back again.'

Cassandra gave an exaggerated sigh. 'Then I suppose I'll have to give you a hand.'

All the same, her legs felt oddly stiff as she walked over to him. For some reason, she didn't want to touch him again just yet, not after last night. Not that anything had happened, she reminded herself a little irritably. And Jared didn't even remember it at all! At least, she didn't *think* he did. It was so hard to be sure of anything with this man.

He got to his feet, and then rested one arm firmly against her shoulder. She was surprised at how much of his weight he allowed her to take. He really must be feeling rough, she told herself rather guiltily. Then there wasn't much chance to think of anything else. Despite his leanness, he was no lightweight, and by the time he was safely back in bed again she was breathing heavily and her shoulder felt half-crushed.

'From now on, you'd better stay in that bed until you feel strong enough to get around under your own steam,' she said acidly. 'I'm not a weight-lifter!'

'No, you're much too pretty,' he murmured sleepily, to her astonishment. He gave a huge yawn. 'Excuse my bad manners, but I'm afraid I'm going straight back to sleep again.'

'What about that drink you wanted?'

But there wasn't any reply; he was already dead to the world. Cassandra looked down at him rather worriedly. Was it natural for him to sleep so much, and so very soundly? She didn't know. She supposed a doctor would be able to tell her—in fact, Jared should probably have had some kind of medical help—but she had no idea where to get hold of one. In the end, she gave a small shrug. She supposed she would just have to let nature take its course. At least he didn't seem to be getting any worse. He might still be physically weak, but his mind was definitely clear—perhaps even clearer than he was letting on. Sometimes, his voice sounded a little slurred, but his eyes rarely lost their lucid brightness.

Much to her surprise, the next couple of days passed without too much hassle. Jared still slept a great deal, and even when he was awake he didn't seem to have enough energy to indulge in his favourite game of deliberately provoking her. Then, at the end of the week, she came shuffling downstairs late in the morning, yawning because she had over-slept, and found Jared standing by the window in the drawing-room. He was fully dressed, looked alarmingly alert, and gave the impression that he had already been up for a couple of hours.

'Yesterday you couldn't even get out of bed,' she

said rather accusingly. 'And now you look as if you could run the four-minute mile. Have you been putting it on the last couple of days? Did you enjoy having me running around after you? Perhaps you decided that you'd make it last a bit longer!'

'What a very suspicious mind you have,' Jared remarked. 'Do you really think I'd try and take advantage of you, Miss Cassandra Gregory?'

She decided to ignore the gentle taunt behind his words. This morning, she didn't feel up to a battle of words.

'I just didn't expect to see you standing there,' she said, rather crossly. 'You gave me quite a fright!'

His eyebrows lifted a fraction. 'Do you find me so very alarming?'

'Considering everything that's happened, I'd have thought that was one question that didn't need answering,' she retorted.

Jared seated himself comfortably in the nearest chair. 'If I have that sort of effect on you, then why are you here?'

'I've already told you that,' she muttered, suddenly feeling unexpectedly flustered. 'You were too ill to be left on your own.'

'But you didn't have any qualms about walking out on me that first night I was taken ill,' he reminded her. 'So—what happened in London to make you change your mind, and come back?'

Oh, this man was just too damned sharp! she thought to herself irritably. He always seemed to know *everything*.

She walked further into the room and flung herself down in the chair opposite him. She felt tired and edgy—not that there was anything new in that! She seemed to have felt that way ever since she had first set eyes on Jared Sinclair.

Because she didn't want to look at him, she stared out of the window instead. The view didn't cheer her any, though. It was a dark, gloomy morning, with mist swirling down from the mountains and a grey haze draining every trace of colour from the ground and the sky. The house itself felt even colder and bleaker than usual, and she was sure that the gloomy atmosphere wasn't doing much for her sudden mood of black depression.

'You want to know what happened in London?' she said at last, surprising even herself that she was willing to talk to him about it. 'I spoke to my father. That's what happened.'

'I thought that might have been it.' Jared's own voice was as cool as ever.

'Of course you did!' she snapped back, with another swift flare of pure irritation. 'You know everything, don't you?'

'It might seem like that at times,' he replied, with an unexpected glint of humour. 'But I'm no more clairvoyant than anyone else. It's just that I'm beginning to understand quite a lot about you, Casandra.'

She didn't like it when he used her name in that familiar way. It was too—personal. It somehow gave the impression that they had been friends for years. Close friends.

'Are you going to tell me what you and your father talked about?' he prompted, as the long silence between them stretched on.

'I doubt if I have to do that,' she replied stiffly. 'I'm sure you can work it out.'

'I'd still like you to tell me yourself.'

'Glenveil Toys, of course,' she got out after another

lengthy pause. 'What else?'

Jared studied her thoughtfully. 'I see,' was all he eventually said, though.

'Do you?' she demanded. 'Do you *really* see?'

'Yes, I think that I do,' he answered, in a much quieter voice. It was a tone Cassandra had never heard him use before, and she glanced at him warily. What was coming next?

'You discovered that what I had told you was basically the truth,' Jared guessed. 'You realised that your father wasn't quite the man you'd thought him to be, and that came as quite a shock. Disillusionment like that always hits you hard. On top of that, you felt guilty about walking out on me when I was ill. In the end, it all got so confused inside your head that you weren't sure what you were doing—or why. All you knew was that you were a Gregory, and that put you under an obligation to try and put everything right. And the only way you could think of to try and make amends was to rush back up here and save my life—even though it didn't actually need saving,' he added, rather drily.

Her head shot up. 'You're making it sound as if I came back here for purely selfish reasons, to salve my own conscience. That the fact that I was worried about you didn't have anything to do with it!'

'I don't suppose it did,' replied Jared calmly. 'Anyway, I would have recovered, whether you were here or not. Having you around to mop my brow and run in and out with hot drinks just made life a little more comfortable, that was all. I didn't actually need you.'

Cassandra stared at him with a kind of appalled fascination. 'You are such an unfeeling man,' she said at last, almost in a whisper.

'I know that.' For an instant, his voice was unexpectedly bleak. 'I've warned you about it several times. Don't expect me to change. I happen to like the way I am right now.'

'You mean it's easier when you don't feel anything?' she challenged.

'Exactly.' As always, there was no anger in his voice. 'But since I don't intend to spend the morning discussing my personal feelings—or lack of them—let's get back to the original subject. Now we've established why you came here, perhaps it's time we moved on to the next question. How long do you intend to stay?'

Since it was something she had avoided thinking about for the last couple of days, she couldn't give him an immediate answer.

'Are you telling me that you want me to leave?' she said finally, in a rather small voice.

'It makes very little difference to me whether you leave or stay here indefinitely,' came Jared's unemotional reply.

For some reason, his indifference abruptly stung. 'You *are* feeling better this morning, aren't you?' she snapped back at him. 'It's like talking to a blank wall!'

He simply shrugged. 'If you don't want to carry on with this conversation right now, we can always continue it at some other time.'

'What's the point?' she said, with more than a touch of sarcasm. 'I don't suppose your attitude will have changed one jot by then.'

'Probably not. So, let's get back to the point in hand. How long am I going to have the pleasure of your company?'

'I don't know,' she admitted at last, rather grudgingly. 'I—need time to think things over.'

And that, at least, was the truth. She had absolutely no idea what she was going to do next. Coming up here had been a fairly impulsive decision, and staying had seemed inevitable once she had discovered how ill Jared was. He seemed to have made a miraculous recovery now, though. Obviously, once the fever had passed, he had only needed a couple of days of complete rest in order to get right back on his feet again. She wasn't needed any longer—so, where did she go from here?

It was a question that she just couldn't seem to answer right now. She felt too tired, too jaded, too—— What was the word Jared had used? Disillusioned—yes, that was it. Wanting to break free of her stifling relationship with her father was one thing. To have it severed so abruptly—and painfully—was something else. She needed time to get used to the idea, to come to terms with the fact that her father was—— Was what? she wondered grimly, remembering Jared's accusations against him, and the way her father had proudly boasted of how he had taken advantage of the tragedy that had hit Jared's life. Not a man she could love—or perhaps even like.

She looked up, and found Jared was still watching her closely. She wished he wouldn't do that! She hated being watched, and especially by him.

Rather too quickly, she got to her feet. 'I'm going out,' she announced abruptly.

Jared glanced out of the window, at the gathering mist. 'In this? You'll get lost.'

'Then you won't be bothered with my company any more, will you?' she retorted. 'I dare say you'll find that a great relief.'

'It'll certainly be a great deal more peaceful around here,' he agreed amicably. His gaze drifted over her. 'At least you're more sensibly dressed this time,' he added. 'I won't have to worry about you breaking an ankle in ridiculous stiletto heels, or catching pneumonia through wearing entirely unsuitable clothes.'

'If I remember rightly, *you're* the one who's had pneumonia,' she reminded him. 'And *you're* the one who got the 'flu, and became ill. If anyone needs to look after themselves, I don't think that it's me!'

To her surprise, he actually looked amused. 'I think you're probably right,' he agreed, almost cheerfully. 'But all the same, if you're not back in an hour, I intend to raise the alarm. The mountains and the loch might look very picturesque, but this area can also be highly dangerous if you get lost.'

'How are you going to raise the alarm?' she demanded. 'Send for help by carrier pigeon?'

'I thought using the phone might be more practical.'

'But you don't have a phone.'

Jared's mouth curved into a faint but genuine smile. It was such an unexpected reaction that Cassandra actually blinked in pure astonishment.

'Just because you didn't find a phone when you were here on your first—visit,' he said, a second flicker of amusement showing in his eyes, 'it doesn't mean that I don't have one. I simply unplugged it, and put it somewhere you wouldn't find it.' Then his expression changed back to its familiar blandness. 'One hour,' he reminded her.

Cassandra got to her feet and rather stiffly walked out without answering him. She pulled down her thick anorak from the coat-stand in the draughty entrance hall, wriggled into it, and then went out, slamming the front door loudly behind her. He needn't think he could dictate what she could or couldn't do, because he would soon find out she wouldn't stand for it. She would stay out for as long as she pleased—and if he alerted every rescue service in Scotland unnecessarily then he would look the fool, not her!

The mist swirled round her damply as she tramped down the path, and a fine drizzle was beginning to fall. Everything had turned to a dismal shade of grey, which exactly matched her mood. If you needed cheering up, this was definitely *not* the place to come to, she decided with a dark grimace.

Since the grass was wet and slippery, she decided to stick to the road. There was no point in risking a twisted ankle. She certainly didn't want to be immobile—that would give Jared Sinclair too many advantages, and she had the feeling that he had more than enough of those already.

She went the way she had gone before, on the day she had tried to escape from Glenveil. Since she was wearing flat-soled shoes, she could walk much more quickly and easily this time, and it wasn't long before the derelict cottage came into view. She gave a wry sigh as she remembered how pleased she had been to see it that first time; and how bitterly disappointed when she had found it was uninhabited.

After a couple of minutes, she turned back. Her gaze drifted towards the road, and it was a few moments before she realised she was half expecting to see Jared's old car there again, with his shadowy figure inside, waiting to take her back to Glenveil.

'Idiot!' she muttered under her breath, annoyed with herself for being so stupid.

A glance at her watch told her she had been out for a little over half an hour. If she started back for Glenveil now, she would just make it before the hour was up.

You don't have to go, she told herself firmly. He doesn't have any right to tell you what you can do, or how long you can stay out, as if you were a rather tiresome child he has to keep an eye on.

But, somehow, her feet had already started walking back in that direction. And she had to admit it was cold, and unpleasantly damp. There wasn't any point in staying out just to spite him.

By the time she reached the house, she was so chilled that Glenveil looked almost inviting. She opened the front door, kicked off her wet shoes and hauled off her anorak, and then turned round to find Jared standing in the doorway.

'Perfect timing,' he complimented her. 'You made it with two minutes to spare.'

Cassandra shot him a black look. 'I think I liked you better when you were in bed, semi-conscious!'

'Why?' he probed. 'Because you find me hard to take? Or because it gave you a perfect excuse to stay? And you do want to stay, don't you, Cassandra?' he finished softly. 'I think you knew that even before you went out. You didn't need a long walk to help you make up your mind.'

'If it isn't inconvenient, I'd like to remain here for just a few more days,' she agreed, in a rather stiff voice. 'I can pay you rent, of course, if you want to make the whole thing formal. I don't know what the going rate is for a freezing cold barn of a place in the middle of nowhere, but I'll pay you whatever you think is fair.'

'*Anything* I ask?' he drawled.

But she was getting to know him better by now, and she refused to rise to the bait.

'Any reasonable sum of money,' she replied coolly.

'Sometimes you can be very disappointing, Miss Cassandra Gregory,' he murmured. 'Did you know that?' Then he levered himself away from the doorway, and she realised he had been leaning against it because he was suddenly almost too tired to stand up unaided. 'We'll discuss this at some other time,' he said, stifling a huge yawn. 'I think I need to be clear-headed when we settle the precise terms.' His eyes briefly gleamed. 'But we will discuss them,' he promised. And, before she had time to get alarmed, he turned and walked away.

Cassandra didn't see him again that day. She didn't know if he spent it sleeping, or just resting in his room. Nor did she particularly care. It was just a relief to be free of his company for a while. Sometimes, she felt confident that she could cope with him. Other times, she was much less sure. And today, for some reason, she knew that she couldn't cope at all.

Next morning, Jared was not only up and around, but he also had enough energy to get the generator working again, so that they once more had electricity. And when Cassandra turned on the tap, hot water came gushing out. The boiler had been lit! She was so delighted that she had a sudden impulse to throw her arms around Jared, and give him a hug of appreciation. Better not, she warned herself wryly. He might take it entirely the wrong way. Instead, she went upstairs and indulged in the luxury of a long, hot bath.

The weekend passed with surprisingly few problems. The weather improved slightly, and that in turn seemed to affect her own mood, which brightened considerably. She didn't see a great deal of Jared—he spent quite a lot of time stretched out in a comfortable chair in the library, either reading or sleeping—and that suited her down to the ground. Just by being in the same room with her, he could make her feel uneasy. She didn't know why, but she was certain she wasn't imagining her reaction.

On Sunday evening, she sat in the drawing-room for a couple of hours, enjoying the warmth from the fire as she listened to a play on the radio. When the play finally finished, she got up, yawned, and decided to amble upstairs.

She put a guard around the fire, then left the drawing-room. As she closed the door behind her, though, she heard another door opening and closing a little further along the hallway. She turned her head, and her muscles instinctively tensed as she saw Jared walking towards her.

'Going up to bed?' he asked.

His tone was very casual, and she told herself there was absolutely no need to get alarmed.

'Yes,' she said, rather guardedly.

He didn't say anything else, but simply fell into step beside her as she went up the stairs.

When they reached the first floor landing, she paused for a moment.

'Er—goodnight,' she said, wishing she felt—and sounded!—less awkward.

Jared didn't move, though. Instead, he looked at her speculatively.

'You seem a little edgy,' he remarked at last. 'It makes me wonder——'

'Wonder what?' she asked uneasily. Then, almost immediately, she wished she hadn't asked that question.

'Just what it is you want from me,' Jared replied, his silver gaze still resting on her with cool thoughtfulness.

'Nothing!' she shot back at once.

'Then why don't you want to leave Glenveil?'

It seemed a perfectly reasonable question, so she couldn't figure out why she couldn't think of an equally reasonable answer.

'What on earth would I want from you?' she demanded.

'I don't know. But I wondered if perhaps it was this——'

He didn't give the impression that he had moved very fast, and yet she didn't seem to have any chance to back away before his lips closed over hers. The kiss that followed was very similar to the one he had given her once before—very expert, frighteningly enjoyable, and yet curiously unemotional. She was quite certain that, although he was enjoying the pleasant physical sensations it was arousing, it went no further than that.

She just wished that she could say the same thing. She definitely *wasn't* reacting coolly. Her heart was thumping wildly, her legs were shaking gently, and her skin was beginning to feel distinctly flushed.

'I thought you weren't interested——' she somehow managed to get out, as the pressure of his lips eased off a fraction.

'Did I say that?' he murmured. 'Yes, I believe I did. And I probably meant it, at the time.'

Cassandra's alarm deepened. They were alone in this house—and he was a strong man. 'But you've changed your mind?' she whispered shakily.

Jared's mouth curved into a half-smile. 'There's no need to look so frightened. I'm not about to force you into anything. I'm simply saying that, although I might be fairly indifferent to most things, I'm still capable of enjoying sex for its own sake.' His hand slid down almost casually over the curve of her breast. The sensation caused a deep fluttering that seemed to spread right down to the very pit of Cassandra's stomach, and she only just managed to bite back a small gasp. 'If you feel the same way, we could probably spend a very enjoyable few hours together.'

She meant to say that she certainly did *not* feel like that; although she knew it was pretty old-fashioned, she had never been able to take a casual attitude to sex. The words stuck in her throat, though, as Jared's hand moved again, sliding easily under her jumper and then rubbing lightly and persuasively against her suddenly hardening nipple.

'Or perhaps it's a little more complicated than that,' he went on, in the same conversational tone. 'You seem to have a fairly hostile attitude towards your father at the moment, and this would be the ultimate way of getting back at him, wouldn't it? Sleeping with me? Is that why you wanted to stay?' he asked, apparently not in the least disturbed by the idea. 'To get a rather twisted sort of revenge—your own brand of wild justice?'

Those last couple of remarks finally jerked her out of her lethargy.

'That is a *disgusting* thing to say! Do you think I'd go to bed with you just to—to——'

'To deliberately hurt your father?' Jared finished for her, still in an unperturbed voice. 'You might. I don't know you well enough to know for certain either way. I do know that you like it when I kiss you, though,' he went on, and suddenly his voice was a fraction less cool than it had been a moment ago. 'And I found it surprisingly enjoyable, as well.'

'You did?' she retorted. 'Then all I can say is that you've got a funny way of showing it!'

'What did you expect?' he asked, with one of those rare flashes of amusement that always caught her by surprise. 'A lot of heavy breathing and unrestrained passion? I don't seem able to manage that any more. Taking it more slowly and coolly doesn't make it any less pleasant, though,' he went on almost lazily. His hand was back at her breast again now, moving almost teasingly, but still startling her into another quick flare of response. 'Interested in finding out just how good it can be?' he invited.

'No!' This time, she did actually manage to get the word out. Nor did she have to say it twice. Jared let go of her at once, and then smoothly moved away from her.

'Then we'll each keep our secrets for a while longer,' he said easily. 'Goodnight, Cassandra.'

He turned and walked into his own room. It wasn't until the door had actually closed behind him, though, that Cassandra found herself capable of moving again. And even then, her legs felt horribly shaky as she headed towards her own bedroom.

CHAPTER SIX

CASSANDRA spent yet another restless night. Annoyed at not being able to sleep, she tossed around in the four-poster bed and told herself that it was the cold that was keeping her awake. The room felt like an ice-box, and she was sure the temperature outside had to be close to freezing. Much more of this, and she would have ice-cubes clinking around in her veins!

She got up as soon as it began to get light. After pulling on a thick cardigan, she padded over to the window and found that a light patterning of frost covered the corners of the glass.

'I *knew* it was freezing,' she muttered under her breath.

She had to admit that it looked pretty spectacular outside, though. Everything glittered beneath its thin coating of frost, and the air was very still and clear.

Deciding that she would appreciate it even more if she felt warm, she shoved her feet into a pair of slippers and headed downstairs, towards the kitchen. What she needed right now was a piping hot drink.

She pushed open the kitchen door, and then caught her breath in surprise. Jared had got there before her. He was sitting at the table, fully dressed and looking alarmingly alert. Cassandra gave a silent groan. Last night was still uncomfortably fresh and vivid in her memory. She had been hoping for some time to herself, so she could think it over, try and work out exactly what it had meant, before having to face Jared again.

'Want some coffee?' he offered, as she hovered uncertainly in the doorway.

'Er—yes,' she said a little warily.

She slid into the seat opposite him, somehow managing to avoid any direct eye contact.

He placed a mug of hot coffee in front of her, finished his own drink, and then sat back comfortably.

'You're going to have to look at me some time,' he remarked at last.

'I'm not scared of you,' she flashed back instantly, annoyed that he so often seemed to know what was going on inside her head.

'No, not scared,' he agreed easily. 'But you're not sure how to cope with the situation. And you're a little worried about what's going to happen next.' His mouth curved into an unexpected smile. 'You're perfectly safe, you know. I never jump on anyone before breakfast.'

'And what about after breakfast?'

'Only by invitation.'

Cassandra lifted her head indignantly. 'But last night, I didn't——'

'Didn't invite me to kiss you?' Jared finished for her, as her voice trailed away to a small splutter. 'Wrong, Cassandra. You didn't actually put it into words, but the invitation was still there.'

'How can you say that?' she said hotly. 'Nothing I said or did gave the *slightest* impression that that was what I—I wanted.'

'Maybe you didn't do it intentionally,' Jared agreed calmly. 'But I was still getting clear signals.'

'Whatever you thought you were getting, you were definitely mistaken!' she insisted vehemently. 'I should know what I did or didn't want.'

His silver gaze regarded her steadily. 'Right now, I think you're so confused that you don't have the slightest idea what you want,' he told her. 'That's why you're still here—you can't even make up your mind whether to leave or not. Or where you should go.'

'All of a sudden, you seem to know a lot about me,' she said furiously.

'And you don't like that?'

'No, I don't!'

'Why not?'

'Because——' Cassandra hesitated. She didn't know why not. She just had the feeling that it definitely wouldn't be a good idea to let this man rummage around in her most private thoughts and feelings. 'I don't like it when people start interfering in my life,' she muttered at last.

Jared shook his head, and a faint smile touched the corners of his mouth. 'Cassandra, it might be worth keeping you around for your entertainment value! You came back here uninvited, had a thoroughly good time ordering me around when I was ill, and now you seem to be considering staying on here indefinitely, even though I haven't actually asked you to stay. Yet you're accusing *me* of interfering in *your* life.'

She hadn't looked at it from that point of view before.

'You mean, you want me to go?' she mumbled.

'I've already told you that you can do exactly as you please. It makes no difference at all to me.'

For a split second, she found herself wishing that

it did make a difference. Then she hurriedly pushed that thought away again. She could do without that sort of complication!

But that still left the main question unanswered. Did she want to pack her things and clear out, or take a chance and stay on for a few more days, despite what had happened last night? It would be crazy to stay, she reminded herself. After all, what did she really know about Jared Sinclair? No one in their right mind would choose to move in with a virtual stranger.

Yet, just now and then, she got the feeling that she was getting to know him extraordinarily well. At least, as well as anyone would ever get to know this extremely self-contained and private man.

Cassandra sighed. She wished she could think straight. At any other time, she was sure she would have been able to reach a sensible and logical decision. She had a cool head and a good brain—so why couldn't she seem to use them?

Because of this man sitting opposite you, whispered a small voice inside her head. One look from him, and you suddenly get totally confused. One touch, and the world seems to turn topsy-turvy.

Which was all the more reason to leave. So, why couldn't she reach that simple decision?

'I suppose the trouble is, I don't really have anywhere else to go at the moment,' she said at last, very reluctantly.

'You don't want to go back to your flat in London?'

'No.' Her answer was immediate. She didn't even have to think about it.

'Why not?'

'Because I don't want to see my father again. Not for a while.' She hated to put it into actual words, but she had the feeling that Jared wouldn't settle for anything less than the truth.

'So you intend to hide away up here?'

'Not hide,' she said, a little annoyed at his faintly taunting tone. 'I'm not a coward! I just need—well, time to think things over.'

His features had taken on that unreadable expression again now. 'To decide if your father's a saint or a villain?'

'I don't suppose he's either of those things,' she muttered. 'Just someone who's made some perfectly human and understandable mistakes.'

Yet even she could hear that her voice was completely lacking in conviction. She knew why, as well. She could still see her father's face as he had openly gloated at his victory over Jared Sinclair. Now that she had seen that unpleasantly ruthless side of him, she doubted she would ever be able to forget it was there. Nor did she think her feelings for him were ever going to be the same again.

'Do you know what I think?' said Jared softly. 'I think that you've got two reasons for wanting to stay here. Firstly, as you said, you don't have anywhere else to go right now. You've run away from your old life, but this is the only place you've got to go at the moment. And secondly, you *want* to be here. It's like a double punishment for your father. You've not only run away from him—you've moved in with a man he despises.'

'He doesn't despise you,' she said in a low voice.

'Oh, yes, he does,' Jared replied with absolute certainty. 'In his eyes, I'm a loser. And your father only has any regard for the winners of this world.'

'You're not a loser!' As soon as she had said it, she was astounded. What on earth had made her blurt

that out? Jared didn't need anyone to jump to his
defence; he was more than capable of looking out for
himself.

'You think not?' His eyes were very clear now, but
still quite untroubled, as if the prospect of being
branded a failure didn't bother him in the least.
'Then why am I hiding away up here, in the middle
of nowhere? Why haven't I made the slightest effort
to try and rebuild my life?'

'Because you need time,' Cassandra said with some
certainty. 'When life knocks you completely flat, you
can't just get up straight away and start over again.
It's like being seriously ill—you have to have a
convalescent period before you can get back on your
feet.'

'What a very apt simile,' he mocked her gently. Yet
there wasn't any underlying sarcasm in his tone.
'And what role do you intend to play? My nurse?'

She flushed. 'You don't need me to prop you up.
In fact, I can see now that you don't really want me
around at all. You're right, I shouldn't have just
dumped myself on you. I'll pack my things together
later, and go.'

'There's no need for that. I dare say I could get
used to having you around.'

His reply astonished her. 'But—you don't actually
want me here, do you?'

Jared gave a brief shrug. 'You need somewhere to
stay at the moment. It might as well be here.'

She suddenly stared at him suspiciously. 'Why are
you being so nice to me all of a sudden?'

'Perhaps I feel that I owe you.'

'For what?'

'I did virtually kidnap you,' he reminded her.

'Yes, you did,' she said with some acerbity. Then

she added, a shade reluctantly, 'But you did have a good reason for behaving the way you did.'

'A court of law probably wouldn't look at it that way. And looking back, I'm willing to concede that I didn't behave altogether rationally.'

Cassandra's gaze rested on him curiously. 'You mean that you wouldn't do the same thing all over again, if you had the chance?'

'That's exactly what I mean. I seem to be looking at things a lot clearer since I've been ill. The way I behaved before——' Jared gave a wry grimace. 'It was the first time in my life I've ever done anything quite that crazy.'

'And to make up for it, you're willing to let me stay here for a while?'

'Something like that.' His silver gaze rested on her levelly. 'Are you going to take up my offer?'

As always, she meant to say no. And, as had happened before, the word just didn't come out. Instead, she somehow found herself nodding.

'I suppose so.'

'That's settled, then.' He didn't look either pleased or displeased. Cassandra felt another wave of irritation at his utter indifference. Then she reminded herself that she ought to be grateful for it. While he felt that way about her, she had absolutely nothing to worry about. They could live like brother and sister, with absolutely no problems.

And what if he decides to kiss you again, like last night? asked a small voice inside her head.

He won't, she told herself firmly. That had been a one-off; a misunderstanding between them that definitely wouldn't happen again. For the next few days, she could concentrate solely on trying to sort out her own life. And Glenveil, in its solitary splen-

dour, was the perfect place to do it. It was the refuge
that she needed right now.

Rather to her surprise, things went as smoothly as
she had hoped. In fact, her only real problem was
boredom. She was used to working hard, and having
virtually every hour of the day filled with problems
that had to be solved, or new ideas that needed
developing. She couldn't seem to adjust to all this
sudden leisure.

She had no idea how Jared spent his time. He
frequently disappeared for long stretches, and
although she supposed he was in some other part of
the house she never tried to follow him or asked him
what he was doing. He had already made it perfectly
clear that he didn't appreciate any probing into his
private life, and she didn't want to do anything to
antagonise him. If she did that, he might change his
mind about letting her stay here, and chuck her out
instead.

One day, though, it finally got too much for her.
When Jared made one of his rare appearances at
lunch, she flung herself down in the seat opposite
him and looked straight at him.

'I'm bored,' she announced.

One of his eyebrows lifted gently. 'And what am I
supposed to do about that?'

'I don't know,' she admitted, rather disconso-
lately.

'Then why bother me with your problems?'

His cool question instantly riled her. 'You're
definitely not the sympathetic type, are you?'

'If you want sympathy, you'd better go somewhere
else,' came his unruffled reply. 'All I ever offered you
was a roof over your head. I didn't offer to provide

entertainment as well.'

Cassandra glared at him. 'No, you didn't, and you're certainly living up to your side of the bargain! Anyway, what do *you* do all day?'

'I don't see that's any of your business.'

Since he had a point there, she bit back a scathing retort. Instead, she tapped her fingers rather impatiently on the table.

'No one's forcing you to stay here,' he reminded her. 'If you're that bored, why not go back to London? Or take yourself off on a holiday somewhere?'

But, for some reason, those alternatives just didn't appeal to her.

A couple of minutes later, she raised her head and looked at him with new thoughtfulness. 'Are you planning on staying here all winter?' she asked.

'I've no idea,' replied Jared. 'I don't plan ahead. I just take each day as it comes.'

'But there's a good chance you'll stay here right through to the spring?' she persisted.

'It's a possibility,' he agreed.

'Then how about letting me make this place more comfortable for you? It's my job, it's what I'm good at,' she said, her voice gaining enthusiasm all the time. 'I could turn Glenveil into a real home, and it wouldn't cost you too much. Unless you decided to go all the way, and have central heating installed,' she added, thinking fast now. 'It would be expensive, but it would be worth it. Just think of it—warmth right through the house! No more woolly jumpers and thick socks, and freezing to death every night because the temperature in those bedrooms plummets practically to zero.'

'No,' said Jared, calmly but very firmly.

Cassandra wrinkled her nose in disappointment. 'You mean you can't afford it?'

'I can afford practically anything I want.' As she shot a look of surprise at him, he went on, 'Along with this house, my uncle left me a small fortune. Unfortunately, it came too late to save Glenveil Toys. I'd already lost my company by then. Or rather, your father had cheated me out of it,' he corrected himself, with a sudden dark frown. 'Now that I don't need it, I've got more money than I know what to do with. There's a certain irony in that, don't you think?'

'You really want to know what I think?' she retorted. 'I think that, since your uncle was so rich, it was a pity he didn't buy himself a more comfortable house!'

'Uncle Angus was always of the opinion that a little physical hardship was good for the soul.'

'Well, it doesn't seem to have done much for yours,' Cassandra muttered. 'In fact, I'm not even sure you've got one.'

'A soul?' Jared echoed, with a ghost of a smile. 'No, probably not.'

'So, what are you going to do with all this money?'

'Perhaps I'll just live in idleness for the rest of my days,' he suggested. 'I could well afford to do that.'

'You might be able to afford it, but I don't think you'll do it,' Cassandra replied at once. 'You're not the type.'

Jared looked at her quizzically. 'You think you know me well enough to know what type I am?'

To her annoyance, she flushed. 'Not really,' she mumbled. Then, to cover her sudden confusion, she looked at him with new belligerence. 'If you're rolling in money, why won't you use some of it to make this place more comfortable?'

'Because I happen to like it exactly the way it is,' he said calmly.

'I suppose you think it's very romantic,' she grumbled. 'Log fires, shadowy corners everywhere, rattling windows and ice-cold draughts. Not to mention the tin bath and candles when the boiler goes out and the generator isn't working! Well, I'm afraid I'm a modern girl. I like double glazing and central heating. Not to mention carpets, instead of freezing stone floors.'

'Which just goes to prove how very incompatible we are,' replied Jared, in the same unperturbed tone.

'Oh, you're impossible!' she snapped in annoyance, getting to her feet and stalking over to the door. 'Or perhaps you just enjoy being contrary. Either way, there are days when you really get on my nerves!'

'No one's forcing you to stick around. You're free to walk out whenever you want.'

Cassandra didn't bother to reply, but simply flounced out of the kitchen. She was afraid that if she stayed there much longer she might give in to the temptation to chuck a plate at him!

She remained in a bad temper for the rest of the day, although she wasn't really sure why. Everything just seemed to be irritating the hell out of her for some reason. Perhaps it was because she didn't have anyone to talk to, she told herself. Jared didn't really count. Apart from the fact that he wasn't around much, he wasn't the world's greatest conversationalist even when he was there. And he was so unreasonable about so many things. He just didn't seem interested in looking at anything from her point of view.

By late evening, though, she had calmed down a little and felt in a better frame of mind. By then, she was also a trifle worried. Rather belatedly, it occurred to her that perhaps it wasn't a very good idea to antagonise Jared. She was only here on sufferance. Any time he liked, he could throw her out.

Although it was the last thing on earth she really wanted to do, she decided that perhaps she had better apologise to him. She hadn't been exactly polite to him at lunch time, and she didn't want things to go too badly wrong between them.

From past experience, she knew that she wasn't much good at apologies. That was why it would be better to get it over and done with tonight. By morning, it might just stick in her throat so much that she wouldn't be able to get it out!

The only problem was, she didn't have the slightest idea where Jared had got to. She hadn't seen him since lunch time. A quick check through the rooms on the ground floor revealed no sign of him, and reluctantly she went up and tapped on his bedroom door. Perhaps he had decided to have an early night.

There was no response to her knock, and when she gingerly eased the door open, she found only an empty room. Frowning now, she made her way back downstairs. He wouldn't have gone out, not this late at night. Anyway, there was nowhere to go. This area was definitely short on entertainment facilities. There wasn't even a pub within walking distance.

That meant he had to be in the house somewhere. There were plenty of rooms where he could hide himself away. If she really wanted to see Jared tonight, then she would just have to check through every one of them until she found him.

It was a rather eerie experience, making her way through the silent corridors of Glenveil, and opening doors which led to rooms which had obviously been unoccupied for years. In the end, even her own shadow was making her jump nervously.

'Get a grip on yourself,' she murmured shakily under her breath. 'What do you think's going to happen? A ghoulie or ghostie jumping out and grabbing you?'

She was at the far end of the house now, in a large turret which had been tacked on at some time in Glenveil's chequered history. A winding stone staircase led up to the room on the upper floor, and it was so dimly lit that she felt a definite reluctance to tackle it.

'Come on, don't be such a coward,' she lectured herself a little impatiently. 'You're not scared of the dark, are you?'

The answer to that was probably yes, she realised with a grimace. All the same, she started up the stairs and hoped she wouldn't bump into Uncle Angus's ghost on its way down!

There was a door at the top, and she stopped outside it, slightly out of breath after the steep climb. This was it, she vowed. If Jared wasn't here, then she would give up looking for him tonight, and head straight back to bed. The apology she intended to offer him would just have to wait until the morning.

She pushed open the door, and then stood there in amazement. The room inside was large and brightly lit, and seemed to have been fixed up as some sort of workshop. There were all sorts of machines dotted around, although she didn't recognise any of them, or have the faintest idea what they did. And at the far end of the room was a workbench, which looked as if it was well used. Cassandra blinked. What was this place?

'Well, well,' drawled Jared, 'you're not just a nuisance, you're also a nosy little bitch.'

The sound of his voice made her jump. She hadn't known he was there. In fact, she couldn't see him even now. Then there was a stir of movement from the large armchair on the far side of the room as Jared levered himself out of its depths, and slowly sauntered over to her.

In the past, she had often been annoyed because his eyes were so bland, revealing almost nothing. Tonight, though, they were almost too brilliant. Cassandra found herself wishing they would go back to their more familiar cool remoteness.

He stopped just a couple of feet in front of her. 'I see I'm to be allowed no privacy, not even in my own house.'

She stared back at him a little defiantly. 'You didn't tell me that any part of Glenveil was off bounds.' Then she looked around curiously. 'Is this where you spend most of your time? What do you *do* here?'

'At the moment, I'm drinking myself into a few hours of oblivion,' he said, not very pleasantly. 'And I'd prefer to do it without any interfering female hanging around.'

Her gaze slid past him and fixed instead on the near-empty bottle of spirits standing on the table near his chair.

'You're going to have a hell of a hangover in the morning,' she said bluntly.

'It'll be worth it to get a few hours of sleep without nightmares. Now, are you going to get out of here and let me get on with my drinking session in peace?'

'If that's what you want. But it isn't the answer, you know.'

'I do know that,' Jared replied caustically. 'I'm not completely unintelligent.'

'Then why behave like this? Whatever problems you've got, they'll still be there in the morning. Along with a splitting headache,' she warned.

He took another step forward. 'I don't need any lectures on the subject. And I don't want you hanging around here. Get off to bed—you're boring me.'

But Cassandra wasn't so easily browbeaten. 'So you can finish off the bottle?' she challenged.

'If that's what I want.' His eyes blazed back at her. 'Get out of here, little girl. Or you'll end up out of your depth.'

She sturdily stood her ground. 'I'm not a child. I know what I'm doing.'

Jared's mouth curled into a strange smile. 'But I'm not so sure that I do—which could make it dangerous to stick around.'

She shook her head. 'You don't get rid of me that easily.'

'I'm beginning to think that I'm never going to get rid of you at all. That you're going to be hanging around my bloody neck for the rest of my life!'

'You're the one who got me involved in the first place,' she pointed out. 'If you hadn't come barging into my office that day, lured me up here and then tried to keep me a prisoner, we'd never even have met.'

'If I'd known how it was going to turn out, I'd probably never have come within a hundred miles of you,' Jared growled.

'Do you really mean that?' Her voice came out a bit funny, but to her relief, Jared didn't seem to notice.

'Yes. No. Oh, hell, I'm too drunk to know what I mean,' he muttered.

She looked at him consideringly. 'I've seen people who were falling-down drunk, and they didn't look like you.'

'That's because you've interrupted me before I've had the chance to finish the bottle.'

'It's as well that I did,' she said briskly. 'This would be a very good time to stop, don't you think?'

'No, I do *not* think. Stop interfering, Cassandra. I don't need some damn nursemaid telling me what I can or can't do.'

'Perhaps that's just what you do need,' she insisted. 'Jared, think what you're doing. You're drinking! How on earth can you bear even to touch the stuff after——?'

Her voice abruptly trailed away as she saw the dangerous flicker in his eyes.

'After what?' he prompted, in a voice that was suddenly soft and yet horribly menacing.

She took a very deep breath. 'I know about the accident,' she blurted out, saying it very quickly before her nerve failed her completely. 'I know that it was a drunken driver who caused the—the deaths of your wife and child. If it were me, I couldn't bear to touch alcohol again. I wouldn't even want to look at it. That's why I don't understand——'

'Why I'm getting as drunk as the bastard who killed them?' he finished for her harshly. 'No, I don't suppose you do.' His gaze was still fixed on her with killing intensity. 'Shall I tell you something?' he went on more quietly. 'This is the first time I've touched alcohol since it happened.'

'Then—why tonight?'

'Because sometimes I still find it damn near impossible to live with what happened. Most of the time, I can accept it. I've learnt that you either do that, or you end up totally crazy. But now and then, it just gets too much. And when that happens, I'll try anything to blot it out for a few hours, to get all the nightmarish memories back to an acceptable level. Do you know the best remedy?' He gave a rather twisted smile. 'Sex. Odd, isn't it, that it takes the act of life to blot out the memory of death? Or perhaps it's not very strange at all. Perhaps it's perfectly logical, when you think about it. But since sex isn't available tonight, I thought I'd try alcohol instead.'

Cassandra had never heard him talk like this before. She supposed it was because he wasn't entirely sober. On the other hand, she was sure he was a very long way from being completely drunk. She had the impression that he was a man who could drink a great deal without it having very much effect on him.

Yet there was no denying the raw pain in his voice. Drunk or sober, he was going through some kind of private hell tonight, knocked flat by a whole torrent of haunting memories that were rampaging through his mind, out of control. She felt a desperate sympathy for him, but didn't know what she could do to help.

She came a little further into the room, and then stood there rather helplessly.

'Instead of sex and alcohol, you could always try work,' she said at last, in a low voice. 'My father—he's made a mess of running your company. The new lines aren't selling well, and profits are dropping. There's every chance he could be trying to sell it fairly soon. You could buy it back, start over again——'

'No,' said Jared, with utter finality. 'One thing I've learnt over the last few months—you can't ever go back. You just have to try and carry on from where you are, right here and now.' A cold smile touched his mouth. 'That doesn't mean I couldn't start a brand new company, of course. Do you think that's a good idea?' Before she had a chance to answer, he went on mockingly, 'Perhaps I could call it Cassandra Toys. That's got a rather nice ring to it, don't you think?'

She ignored his taunting tone. 'That sounds fine to me. Would you have anything to sell?'

He gestured expansively towards the workbench. 'What do you think I do up here all day? Sit and gaze at the ceiling?'

'You've been working on a new range of toys?' Her voice was fully alert now. She stared at the workbench, but couldn't make sense of the odd shapes scattered all over it. They certainly didn't look like anything recognisable to her.

Jared saw her puzzled look. 'Watch,' he said briefly. His fingers deftly gathered up the pieces, and in just seconds he had fitted them together. Cassandra gave a small gasp of surprise and delight. Jared was now holding a beautifully detailed model of a spaceship.

'That's fantastic! Have you got any more?'

'About half a dozen, so far. And I'm working on a larger model of a space station——' He rather abruptly broke off at that point, as if he had never meant to say so much.

'If you aren't interested in starting up another

company, why have you been working on these?' Cassandra asked him forthrightly.

'They're not intended for commercial production. They were just a way of passing the time.'

She took the small model of the spaceship from him, and looked at it more closely, fascinated by the perfection of design and detail.

'Why toys?' she asked at last.

'What do you mean?'

'Well—why not computers, electronic gadgets, something more——'

'Adult?' he finished for her.

She gave a very definite shake of her head. 'No, that wasn't what I meant. I don't think anyone could ever accuse you of being immature. I just wondered why you decided to go for toys, instead of any of the other alternatives.'

'I've always enjoyed working on a small scale,' Jared answered after a long pause. 'And there's a great challenge in producing something for young and developing minds. You have to come up with something that stimulates and teaches, and yet is still entertaining. With models like these, that have to be assembled, they have to be hard enough to provide a challenge, and yet not so difficult that the child can't cope with putting it together.'

Cassandra was fascinated. She had never heard him talk like this before.

'You *could* start over again,' she said with certainty. 'Jared, you've got it all going for you. You've got the experience, you know the markets, and you've definitely got the talent.'

'All I lack is the actual incentive.'

She wasn't put off by his negative attitude. 'Perhaps all you need is someone to give you a hefty push.'

'Are you volunteering for that task?'

For the first time, she hesitated. 'No, I suppose not,' she said finally. 'I'm not the right person, am I? I'm a Gregory,' she reminded him. 'I'm the last person you'd want to get involved with, business-wise or—or in any other way,' she finished, a slight flush showing on her face for the first time.

'It's never stopped you interfering before,' Jared commented, a rather caustic note returning to his voice again.

'No, but this is—well, different.' She was almost mumbling now, although she wasn't sure why. Perhaps it was because of the gleam that had suddenly returned to Jared's eyes. She remembered what he had told her about these fits of depression that hit him. His usual cure was sex—and right now, she was the only female around.

'I think I'd better be going,' she went on rather hurriedly. 'It's getting late——'

Jared casually walked towards her. 'I'll come with you.'

'Don't you want to——' Her voice suddenly went squeaky. She cleared her throat, and tried again. 'Don't you want to stay here and finish your drink?'

'There's no point,' he said briefly. 'I could get through a couple of bottles of that stuff, and it still wouldn't make any difference.'

He clicked out the light, and then easily kept up with her as she scuttled rather hastily down the stairs. On her way here, it had been the dark shadows and the silence that she had found rather unnerving. Now she was edgy for an entirely different reason.

All too soon, they were back in the main part of the house. They went up to the first floor together, and when they reached the door to her bedroom, she gripped the handle with a slightly sweaty hand.

'Goodnight,' she said, rather too quickly.

Tired amusement showed on Jared's face, as if he knew exactly what was making her so nervous.

'Goodnight,' he said. Then he began to walk away even before she had started to open her door.

Once she was inside her bedroom, she felt safe—and rather ashamed. All she had been thinking about was herself. As well as that, though, she was surprised to find she felt oddly restless. Almost as if—well, as if she were disappointed that Jared hadn't tried to touch her.

A little stunned by that particular thought, she stood very still in the middle of the room. Don't be crazy, Cassandra, she told herself shakily. He makes you nervous, he rubs you up the wrong way, he——

He fascinated her. Unwillingly, she admitted what she had known for some time. Her reasons for coming back here, and then staying on, were a lot more complicated than she would have liked. She could have gone at any time—she had had a dozen good reasons for going—and yet she was still here.

All the same, Jared Sinclair—*Jared Sinclair*——

Very slowly, she got undressed. She didn't get into bed, though. Instead, she kept thinking about a man who was facing a long and empty night. A man who didn't have anyone to help him get through it.

She stood there for so long that she grew cold, but she didn't even notice the goose-pimples that had begun to creep over her skin. Something inside her seemed to be slowly changing, to be looking at things in an entirely new way. And she couldn't quite get

get used to it.

In the end, she didn't really come to any conscious decision, and yet she found herself moving. And it wasn't towards her own bed. Instead, her feet carried her out of the room and across the landing. Blinking in surprise, she found herself standing outside Jared's door. She started to turn away, but then seemed to get stuck. There wasn't any way she could go but forward.

She still didn't have the slightest idea what she was doing here. All she was sure of was that this was the right thing to do.

She knocked lightly on his door. Then, without waiting for him to reply, she opened it and steadily walked in.

CHAPTER SEVEN

JARED was still fully dressed, and standing by the window. As she stood just inside the doorway, his silver gaze rested on her with cold understanding.

'The sacrificial lamb,' he remarked unpleasantly. 'Very noble of you, Cassandra, but I think I can make it through the night without you.'

Cassandra took absolutely no notice. She was beginning to learn to pay little attention to Jared's more cutting comments. Instead, she listened to his tone of voice—and she could clearly hear the bleakness there.

She moved further into the room, which looked unexpectedly cosy. The fire was burning brightly, and a couple of lamps gave off a soft, warm glow.

'If you don't want to take me to bed, that's fine by me,' she said in a calm voice. 'But I still think you need company, so why not let me stay for a while?'

'Because I don't need you here.'

'I think that you do.' Her gaze remained very steady. 'Either way, you're going to find it pretty hard to get rid of me.'

'So, what else is new?' Jared shot back in exasperation. 'My God, I certainly didn't know what I was taking on when I first got involved with you!'

'Things never turn out the way you expect them to, do they?' she agreed cheerfully. 'By the way, why don't you come and sit by the fire? It must be cold in that half of the room.'

She thought he would probably stay where he was, just to be contrary. After a small snort of impatience, though, he moved away from the window and settled himself in one of the armchairs by the fire. Cassandra hesitated for a few moments. Then she went over and sat on the thick rug, at his feet.

She stared into the flames for a few minutes. Then she said in a quiet voice, 'What was your wife like?'

She couldn't see Jared's face, not without turning her head. And she didn't do that. Instead, she kept staring steadfastly into the dancing flames.

'Not anything like you,' Jared said a little roughly, at last.

'You mean, to look at?'

'Not in any way at all.' He was silent for such a long time that she thought he wasn't going to say anything more. Just when she was wishing that she hadn't given in to the sudden urge to ask that question, though, he began speaking again.

'She was gorgeous—but quite a bitch.' Before Cassandra had time to get over the jolt of shock at his blunt words, he went on harshly, 'You do want the truth, don't you?'

Cassandra swallowed hard. 'Yes,' she said, a little shakily.

'Sure? You might not like it. It isn't a very pleasant little story.'

'I'm listening,' she said evenly.

It was a couple of minutes before he began talking again. 'I first met Adrienne about six years ago. She was the type most men go for, and I was no exception. She was quite something to look at—bright red hair, huge green eyes, and she moved just like a cat. I've never seen anyone so graceful, so supple. But she was like a cat in other ways, as well. Playful one moment, and spitting mad the next. And she certainly liked to use her claws——'

Cassandra gave a faint sigh. 'Why do men always fall for women like that?'

'Perhaps we're masochists at heart,' Jared replied drily. 'Or maybe it's just a question of male pride. We all think that *we're* the one who can tame the tiger.'

'And did you? Tame her, I mean?'

'Of course not. And if it's any consolation, today I wouldn't even try. This is one male who's definitely got wiser as he's grown older. And my tastes have changed, as well. I don't go for all that openly peddled sex any more.'

'Did you——?' Cassandra paused uncertainly.

'Love her?' Jared finished for her. 'At the time, I thought I did. We had an affair that went on for a pretty explosive few months. Then one day, she simply walked out. No warning, no word of goodbye—I just got home and found she'd left.'

Cassandra frowned. 'Why did she go like that?'

'I dare say she found someone who could offer her more than I could. Adrienne was very fond of expensive presents, exotic holidays—all the good things of life.'

'Did you try to find her?'

'Of course, but no one seemed to have the slightest idea where she had gone. And after a while, I was surprised to find that I wasn't even missing her too much. I suppose that says a lot about our relationship. Great in bed, but it didn't have much else going for it.' Jared gave a wry shrug. 'Women probably pick their partners much more carefully. Men rely far too much on their libido. They think if the sex is fine, then the rest will automatically work out as well.'

'If Adrienne walked out on you, how did you come

to marry her?' Cassandra asked.

His tone was much more sombre when he finally replied. 'She waltzed back into my life about three years later. Literally turned up on my doorstep—only this time, she had a young boy in tow. She said she had no money and nowhere to go, and that I had to take the two of them in.'

'And you took her back?' Cassandra said a little incredulously. 'Just like that?'

'No, not just like that,' Jared replied in a dark voice. 'Only after she told me the kid was mine.'

For the first time, Cassandra twisted round so that she could see his face. Then she gave a brief shiver as she saw the grim expression written there.

'You believed her?' she said rather shakily.

'Of course not. At least, not at first. But I could hardly leave the two of them standing there. The kid looked cold and tired—no one with an ounce of pity could have turned him away.' He closed his eyes briefly, as if he could see all over again the young boy standing there, waiting to be let into his home—and his life. 'He was a plain-looking kid,' he said steadily. 'A bit too thin, and he had a runny nose—but he had these bright eyes. You could see just by looking at him that there was a good brain inside that head of his.'

'And was he——?' Cassandra found it extraordinarily difficult to get the words out. 'Was he really yours?'

Jared gave a small gesture with one hand. 'I don't know. Adrienne insisted he was. She said she found out she was pregnant just a couple of weeks after she left me. Apparently, it hadn't been enough to make her want to come back, though. She didn't do that until she was really down on her luck.'

'Wasn't there some way you could prove it one way or the other? Blood tests, or something like that?'

'Probably. It never seemed to matter, though. By the time that kid had been there a couple of weeks, he had me well and truly hooked. He was nothing to look at, but he was so damned bright. And loving. He hadn't had much of a life, always on the move, and no real stability, but he hadn't let it get to him. He just took each day as it came, and got absolutely everything he could out of it. I grew to really love that kid——'

'And so you married Adrienne,' Cassandra said quietly.

'The boy needed a settled, stable home. I knew I could give him that. What was I meant to do?' Jared challenged with sudden fierceness. 'Just kick him out? Could *you* have done it?'

'No, I don't suppose I could,' she admitted in a low voice. 'But marriage to Adrienne—wasn't there some other way?'

'No,' Jared said flatly. 'The boy needed something permanent, not some arrangement that could fall apart at any moment.'

'And what about Adrienne? Did she need a lot of persuading?'

Jared gave a rather grim smile. 'None at all. Things hadn't been going too well for her. The kind of men she liked—the well-off, the well-connected—began to shy away once they found she had a child in tow. My offer of marriage was the best she'd had for a couple of years. She jumped at it. And for a while, things didn't go too badly. We both made an effort—for our own sake, as well as the boy's. She couldn't keep it up, though. Eventually, there were other men. And she did her damnedest to run us into debt, with her endless extravagances.'

Cassandra looked at him with sudden comprehension. 'Was that why there was so little money to spare when Glenveil Toys began to run into trouble?'

'Yes. I was still paying off the overdrafts she'd run up.' Jared shrugged. 'Not that it really mattered. Adrienne and the boy were dead by then, wiped out by a drunken slob who thought he could drink and drive. Nothing seemed particularly important after that for a very long while.'

She bowed her head so that he couldn't see the sudden brightness in her eyes. How on earth could she ever have thought him a cold man? she wondered. He had loved that child so much that he had locked himself into a loveless marriage just so he could provide a stable home for the boy. Would an unfeeling man have done something like that? No, he definitely wouldn't!

'God knows why I'm rambling on like this,' Jared went on roughly. 'I don't suppose you're interested.'

At that, her head shot up again. 'How can you say that?'

'Because it isn't your problem. You don't have to live with the memories. Or try to find some very good reason for bothering to get up in the morning.'

'You get up because you have to keep going. And forward! You're the one who said you couldn't ever go back,' she reminded him. 'Remember?'

'I've said a lot of damned stupid things this evening,' he growled. 'Anyway, saying something is one thing. Doing it is something else again.' Without warning, he suddenly got to his feet. 'I've had enough for tonight. You'd better get back to your own room before I get completely maudlin.'

Cassandra got up but, instead of leaving, she went

to stand in front of him.

'You shouldn't be on your own tonight,' she said in a steady voice.

Jared stared back at her with those queer silver eyes of his. '*I* know that. But only a fool would volunteer to stay with me in the mood I'm in right now.'

She held his gaze unwaveringly. 'Then you'd better call me a fool.'

For an instant, his own eyes flickered and changed. Then they became deliberately blank. 'No, Cassandra.'

Infuriated by the way he was beginning to retreat from her again, she caught hold of his arms and shook him.

'Don't *do* that! You make me so mad when you just shut me out. What are you going to do? Live the rest of your life in this house in the middle of nowhere? Shut out the entire world? Never get involved with anyone again because it *hurts* when you love someone, and then have them snatched away from you?' She glared up at him fiercely. 'You said that boy of yours had guts. Well, it's a pity that the same thing can't be said for his father!'

Jared's face grew dangerously dark. 'How dare you say something like that?' he said, in a voice that was soft, and yet frightened her half to death.

She ignored the fact that her legs had begun to shake. 'Why not?' she challenged. 'Do you know what I think? I think that you're beginning to like me. That you let me stay because you enjoy having me around. Remember when you kissed me the other night? You said it was because I wanted it. Well, I think that *you* wanted it, too. Only you're too damned stubborn to admit it.' She paused and took a steadying breath. 'So—who's going to be the winner tonight?' she said more quietly. 'The past, or the present?'

'You don't have the slightest idea what you'd be getting into,' he said flatly.

'Then tell me.'

'I've had far too much to drink. And tonight, my nerves feel shot to hell. When I'm like this, I'm in no mood to be careful or considerate. I just take what I want—what I need—and to hell with everything else.' His eyes bored down into her. 'Is that really what you want?'

Cassandra couldn't give him an answer. No, she didn't want it to be the way he had described it. But yes, she did want to be with this man tonight. She didn't understand it, she couldn't explain it, but she knew without a shadow of doubt that her life had just completely changed course. Nothing was ever going to be quite the same again.

When she didn't reply, Jared stared at her for a very long time. Then he gave an oddly helpless movement of his shoulders. 'All right,' he said in a low voice. 'Let's try just one kiss, and see how it goes. But you'd better make up your mind pretty fast,' he warned. 'By the time we get to the second kiss, it'll probably be too late for you to change your mind.'

His mouth was as demanding as he had promised it would be—and she didn't care. As he moved forward more forcefully, she slid her arms around his neck to help keep her balance. His hair grazed the back of her fingers, and the light yet vivid sensation made her sigh softly with wonder.

Jared took a quick, deep breath, then raised his head. 'Scared yet?' he challenged softly. 'Want to back out?'

She gave a small yet definite shake of her head. She had the impression that Jared was both surprised —and pleased. 'Well, don't say I didn't warn you——' he growled.

With ease, he picked her up and carried her over to the bed. She shivered for an instant, but it was only because the sheets were cold against her skin. Jared's hands weren't cold, though. Nor were his lips. Her nightdress was disposed of in just seconds; then he slid easily out of his own clothes.

Her hand traced the outline of his body, as if it were something quite magical. He gave a brief shudder, and then caught hold of her wrist. 'No more,' he instructed a little roughly. 'From now on, I'll do the touching.'

And, despite what he had said earlier, he didn't move too fast or too greedily. Instead, he turned his exploration of her into a journey of tormentingly constant pleasure. Cassandra bit her lip, and tried not to groan out loud. She could hardly believe that this was happening, that she was sharing Jared Sinclair's bed. And most of all, she couldn't believe the shivering delight that he was forcing her to experience. His mouth ranged freely over her from head to toe, allowing her no privacy, tasting and taking, but giving generously in return.

His movements became more intense, and she felt his body stiffen with the delicious tension of holding back for far longer than he had wanted or intended. Making no concessions to her own inexperience, his tongue took outrageous liberties, while his hands roamed restlessly, causing total chaos among all her nerve-ends.

'Jared!' she muttered in sudden shock at one point. But he took absolutely no notice, and the new waves of pleasure that rushed through her body sent her tumbling into a breathless silence.

His breathing was harsh and fast now, and his own body slippery with sweat, so his skin moved easily against hers as he slid closer, letting his weight bruise and crush her. The different streams of fiery delight running through her began to gather together into one deep, growing ache which was fast becoming intolerable. But Jared seemed to know exactly how she was feeling—and he most certainly knew what to do about it.

She clung to him tightly, as if he were the only thing that was real in a world that had suddenly gone crazy. He didn't seem to care, though—in fact, he seemed to like it. Then he murmured something huskily in her ear. She didn't catch the words, but it didn't matter. His tone of voice was enough to tell her that he had already waited too long, that he needed her *now*——

And, if the world had seemed crazy before, then complete chaos reigned now as every part of her began to fly apart. Jared's own shivering response only added to the whirling tumult, which snatched away her breath, her sanity, and her very soul. Her body dissolved into his, sharing his flood of pleasure and echoing his groan of unbearable delight.

For a long while afterwards, she felt as if she were floating in an odd sort of limbo. And she had the impression that Jared was drifting right alongside her, oddly at peace for once in his life. It seemed to take for ever for everything to return to normal. Eventually, though, she felt herself come back to earth with a gentle bump. And, at the same moment, Jared lifted himself on to one elbow and looked down at her consideringly.

'Why is it that when you're around, nothing turns out quite the way I expected?' he said softly.

Cassandra shook her head slowly, still feeling dazed. 'I don't know,' she whispered. Then she stared up at him a little anxiously. 'Do you think that you'll be able to sleep all right now? With no bad dreams?'

A slow smile crossed his face. 'Yes, I think that I probably could,' he agreed. 'But I don't think that I want to.'

She tried to swallow, but her throat was suddenly too dry.

'You—you don't?'

'Definitely not,' he confirmed. One of his fingers gently tickled the underside of her breast in a gentle caress. 'Do you?'

Cassandra was rather amazed to find that she didn't. In fact, this was turning out to be the most astonishing night of her life.

'Well, since we're both so wide awake, maybe we ought to try and find some way of passing the next couple of hours,' Jared remarked. 'Any suggestions?'

'Perhaps you could begin by kissing me again,' Cassandra said hopefully. 'That might lead to all sorts of interesting possibilities.'

'So it might,' he agreed.

And, before the kiss was even half-way through, neither of them were in any doubt as to how they wanted to spend the rest of the night.

Jared was the one who finally fell asleep first. Cassandra lay awake for quite a while longer, listening to his quiet, even breathing and trying to work out exactly how this had happened. Because she had felt sorry for him? Yes, she had. But she certainly hadn't jumped straight into his bed out of sympathy. That left one other possibility. Because she couldn't quite believe it, though, she shied edgily away from it. Jared Sinclair would be such a very difficult man to love. Only a real masochist would be mad enough to fall for him.

Deciding that she would think about it some more in the morning, when her brain would hopefully be working normally again, she closed her own eyes and was soon sleeping peacefully.

When she woke up again, the room was filled with bright daylight. She stretched luxuriously, then she abruptly remembered everything that had happened last night, and her eyes flew wide open with shock.

Very cautiously, she turned her head. Then she gave a small sigh that was a mixture of relief and disappointment. The bed beside her was empty. Jared was already up.

At least it gave her time to try and work out how she felt about the situation. The only trouble was, no matter how long and hard she thought about it, she couldn't reach any sensible or logical conclusions. All that kept popping into her head were deliciously vivid pictures from last night, echoes of physical sensations that she couldn't quite believe had really happened, but which her still-tingling nerve-ends told her most definitely had.

You've got to think straight! she told herself a little despairingly. She just couldn't seem to manage it, though.

Rather shakily, she swung herself off the bed and pulled on her nightdress. Where was Jared? she wondered, with a first touch of unease.

She opened the bedroom door, but the house seemed quite silent. Automatically, she began to head towards her own room, intending to put on a dressing-gown before she went downstairs. Then she stopped and gave a rueful smile. What was the point? She was never again going to be able to act the prude in front of Jared!

She finally found him in the drawing-room, sitting by the window, staring out at the loch and the mountains.

'Er—hello,' she said, suddenly feeling unexpectedly nervous. 'How are you this morning?'

'Sober,' he replied briefly. He turned his head, meeting her gaze full on. 'And you?'

'I'm fine.' Then, when he looked a little disbelieving, she added quickly, 'I really am. More than fine, in fact.'

'No regrets?'

'*Regrets*?' she echoed disbelievingly. 'How can you possibly say that? Even think it?'

Jared shrugged. 'Things which seem a good idea in the middle of the night often don't seem quite so attractive in the cold light of day.'

She looked at him with new wariness. 'What exactly are you trying to say?'

'Just that I don't think either of us should let ourselves be carried away by some rather enjoyable fun and frolics in bed.' His tone was very flat, and all the old remoteness was back in his silver eyes again. It was as if he were quite deliberately distancing himself from her, refusing to acknowledge that anything of the least importance had happened between them.

'Jared, *stop* it!' she said furiously. 'You're not going to go back to behaving like some kind of—of robot.'

'Why not?' he said evenly. 'Most of the time, that's exactly what I feel like.'

Cassandra looked at him with sudden pain. 'I

didn't go to bed with a robot last night! Or do you have to get drunk to behave like a human being?' she challenged in a brittle voice.

'Perhaps I do.' He lifted his head and stared straight back at her. 'Maybe this would be a good time to cut your losses and run. Stay here, and you'll probably end up with nothing except a lot of grief. I don't know that I'm ever going to be able to give you what you want from me.'

She couldn't believe he was saying this. Not after everything they had shared last night.

'Perhaps I'd be willing to settle for whatever's on offer,' she said at last, in a low and rather unsteady voice.

'No,' Jared answered at once, in an unexpectedly hard tone. 'You deserve more than that. And I want to be fair to you, Cassandra.'

His use of her name somehow hit her harder than all his previous words. She remembered how he had muttered it during the long hours of darkness, making it sound as if it were the only thing he wanted to say.

'Well, none of this seems very fair to me!' she got out in a choked mutter.

For the first time, Jared's own eyes came alive. They glittered brightly as they fixed on her. Then he got to his feet and prowled around, as if he suddenly found it quite impossible to keep still.

'Why the hell can't you understand?' he growled fiercely. 'Last night was good—in fact, it was a whole lot more than I ever expected—but it hasn't made a damn bit of difference. I'm still *exactly* the same person I was before.'

'I don't believe that,' Cassandra said stubbornly.

'If you want to go on deluding yourself, that's your

problem,' came his taut reply. 'And mine is trying to
do something about this mess I've got us both into,'
he went on in dark mutter.

'Why won't you face up to the fact that you've only
got one problem?' she flung at him rather shrilly.
'And that's admitting you're starting to feel things
again. That part of you is beginning to come alive.'

'I will not!' he thundered back at her. 'Nor will I let
you force me into it!' He looked as if he wanted to
shake her violently, but at the last moment he pulled
back, deliberately stopping himself from touching
her. 'Damn you!' he said furiously. 'When are you
going to stop interfering in my life?'

He strode out of the room, leaving her standing
there, shaking quite uncontrollably. When she had
first woken up this morning, she had never thought
she would have to go through a scene like this.

So much for her dreams of romance! she thought
grimly. Jared obviously didn't know the meaning of
the word.

But when she finally calmed down a fraction she
began to realise that she had never seen Jared quite so
defensive. No matter how vehemently he denied it,
she knew she was beginning to get to him. And, no
matter how much she got hurt in the process, she
intended to go on doing just that. Someone had to
make an all-out effort to bring Jared Sinclair back to
life again, and she was the only one around right now
who had any chance of doing that.

The trouble was, she hadn't reckoned on the
process being so damned painful. She wrapped her
arms around herself, shivering a little now with
reaction. Were her own nerves strong enough to go
through with it? Yes, she told herself stubbornly.
And was he worth all this emotional turmoil? She

didn't even bother to answer that question Although she hadn't realised it until now, she had already gone way past the stage where she was in any doubt over her feelings for Jared Sinclair.

She let out a slightly weary sigh. She supposed she had better go upstairs, take a shower and get dressed. She trailed rather wearily out into the hall, and was just about to head towards the stairs when she heard the sound of a car pulling up outside the house.

Instantly, she frowned. She was sure that Jared wasn't expecting any visitors. Perhaps it was just someone who had got lost, she told herself. Maybe they had decided to knock and ask for directions.

A little flustered, she glanced down at herself. She was still only wearing a nightdress. It was of thick cotton, though, and perfectly decent. And there was absolutely no sign of Jared. Either he hadn't heard the car, or he was deliberately ignoring it. If she didn't open the door, then whoever had just arrived wasn't going to get any reply.

An impatient thumping on the heavy brass knocker made her lift her head slightly irritably.

'All right, I'm coming!'

She hurried over, unbolted and opened the door, and then simply stood there in stunned silence.

Standing on the other side was her father, his florid face looking grim and his mouth set in a bad-tempered line.

'So I was right,' he said in a terse voice. 'You *are* here.'

On top of everything else, it was almost too much. 'What are you doing here?' Cassandra just about managed to get out.

He didn't even bother to answer her. Instead,

he pushed past her and strode into the centre of the hall. 'Where is he?' he demanded angrily. 'I know he's here. This is his house. Hasn't he got the guts to come out and face me?'

Cassandra stared at him in disbelief. 'You've no right to come barging in like this! This is *my* life. It was *my* decision to come here. How dare you follow me, as if I'm some child who's—who's done something wrong?' she finished furiously.

'You are a child,' her father replied shortly. 'And my daughter. I won't let you get involved with a man like him. Sinclair's a failure, a loser. Are you blind, Cassie? Can't you see him for what he is?'

'Yes, I can,' she said, in a suddenly quieter tone of voice. 'And that's exactly why I'm here.'

'But you're not going to stay,' he instructed. 'You're coming home with me.'

She could hardly believe he was saying these things. 'For heaven's sake,' she burst out, 'I'm twenty-two years old! When are you going to admit I'm grown-up? Stop trying to run my life for me?'

Until now, Randolph Gregory had been pacing around the hall, as if he were too wound-up to keep still. Now, though, he turned and looked at her fully for the first time. His eyes darkened as he stared at her, and his mouth twisted into a strange line.

'What's he done to you?' he almost whispered. 'Did he force you into this?'

Cassandra stared back at him uncomprehendingly. Seeing that she didn't know what he was talking about, he suddenly seized hold of one of her arms and marched her over to the ornate mirror that hung at the far end of the hall.

'Look at yourself,' he said in a choked voice. 'My little girl. And look what he's turned you into!'

She gazed at her own reflection, and was a little astounded at the girl who looked back at her. Her pale blonde hair was tangled and tousled, her violet eyes were absolutely huge, and a hectic touch of colour flared across her normally fair skin. She didn't quite recognise herself, which was a slightly unnerving sensation.

'Tell me, Cassie,' demanded her father. 'He did force you, didn't he?'

Before she had a chance to answer him, a cool voice spoke from the foot of the stairs.

'No one could ever force Cassandra into anything. She has a mind of her own, and she's certainly quite capable of using it.'

Neither of them had heard Jared come silently down the stairs.

Randolph Gregory turned and stared at him with a blaze of pure hatred. 'You must have got a great deal of satisfaction out of this. I took your company—so you decided to retaliate by taking away my daughter!'

In contrast to the older man's furious bluster, Jared seemed perfectly relaxed. Cassandra could see the suppressed glint in his eyes, though, and knew that the coolness was no more than a façade. Underneath, Jared was only just managing to hold on to his own fierce temper.

'Why do you keep talking about Cassandra as if she were some kind of possession?' Jared asked steadily. 'She's a fully grown adult, and intelligent enough to run her own affairs.'

'And I suppose we all know the kind of "affairs" that you're referring to,' sneered her father.

'That is *enough*!' Cassandra said furiously, rounding on her father. 'This isn't your house, and you weren't invited here. Why don't you just go, and leave me alone?'

'With a man like him?' Her father gestured contemptuously at Jared. 'Someone who's got nothing left in the world except this tumbledown old ruin?'

'Glenveil is not a ruin!' Cassandra retorted. 'OK, so it isn't some fashionable townhouse, but I happen to like it exactly the way it is.'

She caught Jared's eye at that moment, and flushed brightly as she remembered all the disparaging remarks she had made about Glenveil, and all the times she had complained about the cold, the lack of modern conveniences, the downright bleakness of the place. She hadn't been lying, though. There were days when she could appreciate its romantic qualities, and she understood why Jared didn't want to change it in any way.

'How did you know where to find Cassandra?' Jared asked quietly.

Her father swung round and glared at him. 'I didn't, not for a long time. All I knew was that she seemed to have disappeared off the face of the earth. I went nearly frantic with worry. Then I remembered all those odd questions she'd asked about Glenveil Toys. It was the only lead I had, so I had a private enquiry agent look into it. He finally came up with the interesting piece of information that there was an actual house called Glenveil—and that it belonged to Jared Sinclair.' His face darkened. 'I couldn't believe Cassie would be here, not with you. I didn't know where else to look, though, so I came straight up here—and found the two of you together.'

'Don't make it sound like some Victorian melodrama,' Cassandra said irritably. 'This is the twentieth century, and I'm well over the age of consent.'

'I don't give a damn about that,' her father said, his voice becoming blustering again. 'You're my daughter, and I'm taking you back with me. Get your things—right now!'

Jared took a couple of steps forward, so that he was standing just in front of Cassandra. 'She isn't going anywhere—not unless she wants to.' He turned to Cassandra. 'Do you want to go with your father?'

'No,' she said firmly.

Jared turned back to Randolph Gregory. 'Then I suggest you leave my house.'

For a few moments, Cassandra thought there was going to be a very ugly scene, and she dreaded it. Yet, although Jared hadn't even raised his voice, there was something about him that would have tempted very few men to cross him at that moment.

Her father's colour deepened, and he muttered vehemently under his breath. To Cassandra's astonishment, though, he backed away slightly. He stopped for an instant and threw another black look at Jared, who simply stood there, looking calmly back at him, his silver eyes very steady and very cool. Then her father began to retreat again, heading unwillingly towards the door.

When he reached it, he paused briefly and glared at the two of them. 'I'm going—for now. But don't think I'm going to let it go at this,' he threatened. Then he strode out, slamming the door savagely behind him.

There was a chair near to Cassandra, and she rather abruptly sat down in it as her legs trembled with reaction.

'I should have known he'd come after me,' she

said shakily. 'He's *never* going to let me go. You don't know what it's been like these past few years. It's as if he can hardly bear to let me out of his sight. He's always checking up on me—who I'm with, what I'm doing. When I came here, to Glenveil, I thought I was getting away from him. Only, now he's followed me here!'

Jared gave a faint frown. 'Your father's a very unstable man. And also, I think, an increasingly unbalanced one.'

'I'm sorry he came here,' she muttered. 'I know how you must feel about him. You can't have enjoyed it too much, meeting him face to face like that.'

'No, I didn't enjoy it,' agreed Jared. 'But it didn't actually bother me.' As she lifted her head, he gave a brief smile. 'Yes, I know. It surprised me, as well.'

She slid her fingers into her tangled hair, pushing it back from her forehead. 'I'd better go and get packed,' she said, rather defeatedly. 'He might come back, and I don't want to go through any more scenes like that.'

'Where were you planning on going?' Jared asked, his voice suddenly sounding a little harsh.

'Back to London, I suppose.'

'Where your father can take over your life again?'

She gazed at him angrily. 'I don't see that I've got very much choice! My flat's there, it's where I live and work.' Her flare of defiance died away as quickly as it had sprung up, and she flopped back dejectedly in the chair. 'It's one hell of a mess, isn't it?' she said, with a twisted smile. 'My father wants me too much, and you don't want me at all. I just don't seem able to strike a happy balance.'

Jared's own face altered. 'I didn't say I didn't want

you,' he growled.

'Didn't you?' she challenged. 'It certainly seemed like it to me!'

He suddenly looked as tired as she felt. 'You caught me at a bad moment.'

'That's not hard!' she retorted. 'You don't seem to have many good ones!'

'I didn't have any at all until you came barging into my life.'

A cautious expression crept into her eyes. 'What's that meant to mean?'

'I don't know,' he admitted. 'Right at this moment, the only thing I seem to be perfectly sure of is my own name.' He prowled away from her, as if being too close to her only confused him even further. 'Going back to London would be about the craziest thing you could do right now,' he muttered. 'Why not stay here for a while longer?'

'Just to make you feel better?' she challenged bluntly. 'So you won't suffer from a guilty conscience because you threw me out?'

He rounded on her fiercely. 'Don't push me for my reasons. I can't give you any—I don't even know what they are. All I'm saying is that the invitation's there. Stay if you want to.'

But Cassandra wouldn't let it go at that. 'Is that what you want?' she persisted.

'My God, you're a pushy, irritating woman!' He shot another furious glance at her. 'All right,' he got out at last. 'Yes, damn it! That's what I want. Satisfied?'

Cassandra's face relaxed into her first smile of the day. 'Yes,' she said happily.

And, suddenly, life didn't seem so bad, after all.

CHAPTER EIGHT

DESPITE what Jared had said, though, his attitude towards her remained rather distant over the next couple of days. And he seemed to deliberately shy away from further intimacy. Cassandra wasn't too worried. He couldn't keep it up for ever, she told herself with some certainty. Cracks were already appearing in that wall he had built around himself. One day—and perhaps soon—it would just need a push, and the whole thing would come crumbling down.

At the end of the week, she was clearing away the lunch things when Jared rather restlessly wandered into the kitchen.

'I'm going out for a couple of hours,' he told her.

'For a walk?' Cassandra brightened up. 'Can I come?'

'I'll probably be going quite some way,' he warned. 'You might find it hard to keep up.'

She wasn't put off by his obvious lack of enthusiasm, though. 'You won't lose me,' she assured him.

'I was rather afraid of that,' Jared replied drily. 'All right. Be ready in ten minutes.'

Outside, the weather couldn't quite make up its mind if it were mid-autumn or early winter. One minute, the sun would shine brilliantly through a gap in the clouds, tinging everything with a clear golden light. Then it would disappear again behind a heavy wedge of cloud, the air would suddenly feel chilly, and all the bright colours would fade to much more sombre hues.

Jared didn't keep to the road, but instead headed down towards the loch. Cassandra scrambled rather breathlessly after him, stumbling a little over the uneven ground, and occasionally slipping on the damp grass or tripping over a clump of heather.

When they finally reached the shore of the loch, they both stopped for a few moments and stood there, gazing at the scene. The water was very calm, and reflected the mottled blue and grey of the sky. On the far side, the mountains rose smoothly upwards, patterned with the muted greens of the grass, golden bracken, and the smoky hues of the heather. On the lower slopes, there were darker patches where clumps of Scots pine withstood the worst that the weather could throw against them. The upper slopes were much bleaker, with outcrops of bare rock breaking through to add their own distinctive stripes of colour.

Cassandra wandered right down to the water's edge. It was so clear that she could see the coloured pebbles on the bottom, and, on impulse, she bent down and dipped in her fingers.

'It's freezing!' she gasped a moment later, quickly yanking her hand out again.

'What did you expect?' enquired Jared, a little caustically. 'Hot spa water?'

She scowled at him, but before she had time to think of a suitably acid reply he had set off again, walking so fast that she practically had to run in order to catch up.

He kept going for what seemed like ages, following the shoreline of the loch. After a while, Cassandra heartily began to regret her decision to come with him. She should have realised that he didn't want company today. She would have turned round and gone back to the house if she hadn't been afraid of getting hopelessly lost.

When he finally stopped again, she gave a sigh of relief. 'Are we going back now?' she asked hopefully.

'I don't particularly want to, but I don't think we've got much choice,' he replied. 'The weather's beginning to change.'

She had been so preoccupied watching where she was putting her feet, trying not to fall over loose stones or tangled tussocks of grass, that it was some time since she had had a good look around her. Raising her head, she saw that the blue had completely disappeared from the sky, and heavy swirls of cloud were obscuring the tops of the mountains.

'Is it going to rain?' she asked.

'It looks like it. But probably not for a while.'

'Good,' she said with relief. 'That means I can sit down for five minutes before we head back.'

She collapsed on to a low outcrop of rock, and then stretched out her aching legs.

'I warned you I was going quite some distance,' Jared reminded her.

'I know. Next time you say something like that, make sure I take notice of you.'

He sat down beside her, although she noticed he was careful not to get too close.

'Have you made any plans for the future yet?' he asked, after a rather long silence.

Cassandra glanced at him warily. 'What sort of plans?'

He shrugged. 'I don't really know. But I don't

see that we can go on like this indefinitely.'

'What do you want me to do?'

Again, he gave that infuriatingly non-committal shrug. 'That's rather up to you.'

'Oh, you are a maddening man!' she said in annoyance. 'I don't usually go for the macho type, but sometimes I wish you'd pick me up, sling me over your shoulder, and just *tell* me the way things are going to be!'

Jared's eyes gleamed unexpectedly. 'I could probably manage that, if it's what you really want. But are you sure you'd want to give up your independence that easily? One of the reasons you ran away from your father was so you could begin to live your own life. What's the point in fighting for your freedom if you just go and surrender it to another man?'

She had to admit he had a point there. She *wouldn't* like it if he simply stepped in and began ordering her life around.

'Oh, it's so complicated,' she said rather crossly, at last. 'What I want and don't want—sometimes I think it's quite impossible to sort it all out.'

'And am I complicating things even further?'

'Of course you are. But only because you can't seem to make up your mind what you want, either.'

Jared's expression abruptly altered, but before he had a chance to speak, several large spots of rain hit them.

'I thought you said it wasn't going to rain yet,' Cassandra reminded him.

'Which goes to show that I'm not infallible,' he replied wryly. 'Come on, let's get back to the house.'

The shower eased off fairly quickly, and the sky

lightened again for a while. Then another black cloud began to roll down from the mountains, the far end of the loch became obscured by a thick mist as the weather closed in, and a light drizzle began to sweep over them, quickly increasing to a heavy downpour.

'There's nothing quite as wet as Scottish rain!' Cassandra grumbled breathlessly, as she tried to keep up with Jared's fast pace. Then, a couple of minutes later, she gasped out, 'Jared, will you please slow down? Rushing along like this isn't going to make the slightest bit of difference. I'm already totally soaked. Getting back to the house a few minutes earlier isn't going to make things any better.'

To her relief, he eased up a little. She could keep pace with him quite easily now. Miserably, she squelched along, feeling the rain running down the back of her neck, soaking through her anorak and jeans, and getting right inside her shoes, making them rub uncomfortably.

Jared, on the other hand, didn't seem in the least bothered by the weather. In fact, he almost seemed to be enjoying it. He lifted his face up to the rain, and Cassandra was amazed to see that he was actually smiling.

'What are you looking so happy about?' she asked curiously.

'Nothing in particular. I just feel good.'

She shook her head in amazement. 'You're drenched to the skin and freezing cold—and you feel good?'

He grinned cheerfully. 'It doesn't make a lot of sense, does it?'

'Oh, I don't know. It probably just goes to prove what I've known all along. You're a very contrary man!'

'You mean, I want what I shouldn't have? And turn away from what's good for me?' His tone was still unexpectedly light. 'I dare say you're right. But even the most contrary men sometimes suddenly see sense.'

'Jared, I don't have the slightest idea what you're waffling on about,' she said a little impatiently. 'In fact, right now I don't *want* to know. I'm too wet and cold and completely fed up.'

'You're the one who wanted to come.'

'If you remind me of that one more time, I might hit you,' she threatened. 'How much further have we got to go?'

'About half a mile.' When she groaned, he added, 'Do you want me to chuck you over my shoulder and carry you for the rest of the way, or do you want to make it on your own two independent legs?'

'I'll walk,' she said with some dignity. 'As long as you go at a reasonable speed.'

When Glenveil at last came into view, looming out of the driving rain like a great grey shadow, she let out a huge sigh of relief. Once inside, she shook herself like a wet puppy. Then she stood there, dripping water on to the stone floor.

'I'll make up the fire in the drawing-room,' Jared said. 'You go and find some towels. We need to get dry.'

'I'll be all right, but what about you?' she asked, suddenly looking rather worried. 'Last time you went out in the rain, you ended up in bed with a roaring fever.'

'I'll be all right.' He gave her a gentle push. 'Go and get the towels. And fetch me some dry jeans, if you can find them.'

By the time she trailed back to the drawing-room, clutching an armful of towels and some dry clothes, fresh logs were crackling in the fireplace, sending out an ever-growing circle of heat.

'It would be much more practical to have a hot bath,' Cassandra told him, dumping everything on the floor.

'A nice idea,' agreed Jared. 'Especially if we shared it,' he added with a slightly wicked grin which made her eyebrows shoot up a trifle nervously. 'The only trouble is, there isn't any hot water. I haven't had time to light the boiler today.'

She gave a rather exaggerated sigh. 'Well, if you will go tramping round the countryside, instead of getting on with the important things——'

'Don't nag,' he said comfortably. 'And toss me over a towel.'

Without turning a hair, he stripped off his wet jumper, shirt and denims, and then leisurely towelled himself dry before finally pulling on the dry pair of jeans she had brought him. Cassandra was furious to find herself flushing a very unbecoming shade of red. Jared glanced over at her, noticed it, and gave a sly grin. 'It's a little late for maidenly modesty, isn't it?' he mocked her gently. 'I shouldn't think there's very much you don't know about me by now—including exactly what I look like without clothes.' As he began to towel the worst of the wetness from his hair, he added, 'Shouldn't you get out of your own wet things?'

For some reason, she felt totally awkward and embarrassed. Ridiculous, really, because as he had already reminded her there were very few secrets left between them now. All the same, she wished she could escape to her bedroom, or to the bathroom,

to get herself dry and into some fresh clothes. She
didn't want him to laugh at her, though. Or, worse
than that, to think she was afraid of him. And she
certainly wasn't! she told herself severely. She just
felt—well, a little wary of him all of a sudden. He
seemed—different. There was a new light in his eyes
that she couldn't quite remember seeing before, and,
although she didn't know why, she found it
distinctly disturbing.

She picked up the very largest of the towels,
wound it round her, and then began to wriggle out of
her clothes underneath it. Jared watched the per-
formance with obvious amusement for a couple of
minutes, until she got thoroughly tired of being
caught in the beam of those silvery eyes.

'Will you stop staring at me?' she demanded.

'Of course,' he agreed equably. 'As soon as you
stop behaving like some uptight virgin on her first
date.' And, before she had time to fling an indignant
reply back at him, he strode over and easily whipped
the towel from her shoulders. Then he began to slide
off her wet blouse.

'I can manage by myself——' she began stiffly.

'I know that. But it'll be a lot more fun if I do
it.'

Cassandra stared up at him in astonishment. 'Fun?'
she echoed. 'I didn't think you knew the meaning of
the word!'

'I did forget it for quite a long while,' Jared told her
smoothly. 'But with a little help from you, I think that
I could start to remember exactly what it means.' He
finished removing her blouse, and then his hands
slid down lightly over the curve of her breasts,
brushing against the thin silk of her bra. 'Mmm, that
feels quite dry,' he said thoughtfully. 'So we only

need remove it if we want to. What do you think,
Cassandra?' he invited, in a voice that was fast
growing husky. 'Should we take it off?'

She went to say something, but the words stuck in
her suddenly dry throat. All that came out was a
rather strangled squeak.

'Was that a yes or a no?' he questioned. 'Never
mind, we'll come back to it later. Perhaps we ought to
concentrate on the jeans first. They're definitely wet,
and will have to come off.' He unzipped them, and
dexterously slid the wet denim half-way down her
legs. Then he gave her a firm push, which sent her
toppling back on to the sofa just behind her. Once
she was sitting down, he pulled the jeans right off,
along with her soaking socks.

Cassandra felt oddly weak now. She couldn't even
get out a mutter of protest when Jared reached for a
towel, and began to rub her damp skin. In fact, it
soon dawned on her that she didn't want to protest.
It felt unexpectedly good, the soft, warm texture of
the towel moving up and down her legs, tickling the
soles of her feet, and then gently massaging her
ankles. Then she realised that it only felt good
because Jared *intended* it should feel that way. Her
nerves began to jangle in alarm, and she tried to sit
up, but she couldn't quite seem to make it. Her body
had gone curiously boneless, and she discovered that
it wasn't an altogether unpleasant sensation.

As if he were in no hurry at all, but had all the
time in the world to accomplish whatever it was he
intended, Jared settled himself down comfortably
beside her and didn't touch her again for a couple of
minutes. He was still wearing just the clean, dry
pair of denims he had put on earlier, and as the logs
on the fire caught and blazed, some of the golden

glow reflected on the bare skin of his upper body.

At last, he rather lazily raised one hand and touched a damp strand of her hair.

'It still looks pretty, even when it's wet,' he said appreciatively. Then he twisted the strand round his finger, so that she couldn't move her head without her hair pulling painfully. He shifted a little closer. 'You do realise,' he went on in that same conversational tone, 'that you don't have much choice right now, except to kiss me?'

'I didn't say I wanted a choice,' she got out rather shakily.

'No, you didn't.' He released her hair. 'You can get away, if you want to,' he offered softly.

She didn't move a fraction of an inch, and Jared gave a satisfied grunt.

'There are days when everything seems to go your way. And it's looking as if this might be one of them.'

The kiss that followed was long and intense, and extremely satisfactory for both of them. Cassandra didn't understand Jared's sudden and unexpected change of attitude, but she definitely didn't intend to question it. She was enjoying this far too much.

'You're a seductive piece of baggage,' Jared said at last, with a grin. 'But I suppose you know that perfectly well.'

'No,' she said a little dreamily. 'Tell me about it.'

'I think I'll show you, instead. It'll save time, and we'll both enjoy it a lot more.'

He shifted position so there was room for her to stretch out on the sofa beside him.

'There isn't much room,' Cassandra complained. 'I'm beginning to feel like a sardine!'

'I like it this way. Being wedged up against you

like this is an experience that no man in his right mind would want to miss out on.'

She stared up at him suspiciously. 'You've been in some really odd moods today. And they keep changing so fast—I can't keep up with you.'

'Then don't try,' replied Jared, in an unperturbed tone. 'Just lie back and enjoy the next few minutes.'

'Why?' she said a trifle warily. 'What's going to happen?'

'Well, I thought I'd begin like this——' He left a trail of light, delicious kisses around the base of her throat, taking his time as he explored the tiny hollows, and letting his tongue trace the outline of the underlying bones. 'Then perhaps I'll move on a little——' he continued, his voice still almost conversational, although with a husky undertone now. His fingers drifted down, pausing at the swell of her breasts, and yet making no attempt to release them from the restricting silk of her bra. 'I like silk,' he told her, his fingers rubbing lightly against the soft material. 'I like the way it clings, the way you can see and feel absolutely everything beneath it—including this,' he added, touching the tip of her hardened nipple, and forcing a tiny groan from her.

'Jared——' she muttered, in a helpless voice.

'Lost for words?' He sounded pleased. 'But you don't have to say anything at all. Unless, of course, I do something you don't like.'

'That doesn't seem very likely,' she got out shakily.

'No, it doesn't,' he agreed. His hands returned to her breasts, as if he were fascinated by their warmth and fullness. His fingers moved rather restlessly against the full underswell and then slid back to the upper curves, and suddenly dipped under the lacy edge of her bra.

Feeling his fingertips against her skin was incredibly different from being caressed through the thin silk. Jared seemed equally aware of the new and startling sensations, and an instant later his mouth closed over hers in a kiss that was ferociously demanding. The contrast of that fierce kiss and the still light and tender touch of his fingers was quite exquisite, and Cassandra felt all sense of reality beginning to drift away from her. Without releasing her from the touch of his mouth or hands, he shifted still nearer until they were in contact from head to toe, the pressing closeness of his hard, warm body adding to all the other sensations that were hurtling through her.

Then, without warning, he let go of her again and propped himself up on one elbow, so that he was looking down at her.

'Like that?' he challenged softly.

All she could do was nod numbly.

'So did I. In fact, I think you know perfectly well how much I liked it.' He let his hand rest against the flatness of her stomach. 'But before we go any further, it might be as well to get a few things straight.'

Cassandra gazed at him in growing amazement. 'You want to talk?' she muttered, finally finding her voice. '*Now*?'

Jared gave a faint smile that was a mixture of ruefulness and frustration.

'No, it isn't what I want. But there are a couple of things I need to say——' He stopped abruptly, and lifted his head. 'What was that?'

Cassandra had heard the sound as well. 'It was probably just the wind blowing a door shut. This place is full of draughts.'

Jared frowned. 'Perhaps I'd better check——'

Before he had time to say anything more, though, the door to the drawing-room abruptly crashed open. Cassandra jumped in alarm. Then she swiftly caught her breath as she saw the tall, broad figure that strode into the room.

It was her father. Randolph Gregory looked wild-eyed, and an even higher colour than usual touched his face. He took a quick look at the two of them; then his gaze swivelled to Cassandra and he spat out one short, contemptuous word.

The ugly name he had called her made her begin to shake with a mixture of shame and furious indignation. She felt Jared tense against her; then he lowered his head slightly, so that his mouth was very close to her ear.

'Stay still and keep quiet,' he ordered softly. Then he slowly sat up, pulled on his damp jumper, and got to his feet.

Randolph Gregory glared at Jared with undisguised hatred. 'I always swore I'd kill any man who laid a hand on Cassie,' he hissed in a low voice. 'But I never thought she'd pick a loser like you!'

Although Jared had warned her not to move, Cassandra reached for the towel with shivering fingers, and then pulled it round her bare shoulders. She hadn't dreamt her father would come back like this. And she had never seen him look so out-of-control before, so—so crazy, she admitted to herself, with a frightened shudder.

'You've got to be reasonable,' she said in a hoarse whisper. 'You've got to let me go! I can't stay your little girl for ever.'

Her father didn't even seem to hear her. Instead, he was still staring at Jared with those fixed, hate-filled eyes.

'You're not going to have her,' he said in a rough voice. He reached into his pocket. 'I made up my mind about that after I came here that first time.'

'Jared!' Cassandra cried out in sudden sharp fear. 'He's got a gun!'

'I know.' Jared's own voice was still perfectly steady, and, although his silver gaze was now fixed on the weapon in Randolph Gregory's hand, his stance was very relaxed. Cassandra guessed he was deliberately adopting this attitude, so that he wouldn't provoke or startle her father into using the gun. She didn't know how he was managing to keep so outwardly cool, though. She was shaking unreservedly, and she knew her eyes were huge with fear, and a total disbelief that this could actually be happening.

Almost casually, Jared took a step forward. Immediately, Randolph Gregory responded by raising the gun further. 'One more step, and that'll be it,' he threatened. 'And believe me, it'll be a pleasure. I want to wipe you off the face of the earth for what you've done to my daughter.'

'Do you think all the guns in the world can stop her from falling in love?' asked Jared steadily. Cassandra stiffened a little at that. She had never told Jared she loved him. And yet he knew——

Then she forgot all about it again as her father's finger visibly tightened on the trigger. There was a dark, heavy pounding inside her head, and she knew she was close to passing out. Grimly, she dug her nails deep into her palms. She needed to stay fully conscious, to know what was happening.

'She doesn't love you,' snarled her father. '*I've* always been the only person of any importance in her life. Ever since she was a tiny baby, she's loved me, looked up to me. I'm not going to let someone like you change that.'

'It's already changed,' Cassandra said, fighting hard to keep her voice even. 'Why can't you see that? Accept it?'

'Once you're home with me, you'll forget all about this,' her father said, with total conviction. 'Everything will be the way it was before.'

Cassandra took a shaky breath, ready to argue with him. She didn't get out a single word, though. Jared turned his head and shot a brief look at her, and she read the silent message he sent her very clearly. Her father had gone way past the stage where he was capable of listening to—or even understanding—a reasonable argument. Something inside him had just snapped, and he wasn't seeing things logically any more. He had drifted off into some fantasy world, where he and his daughter would live happily together ever after. All he had to do was get rid of Jared first——

She was ready to cry from sheer terror and the frustration of not being able to get through to her father, to make him realise just how insane this all was. A brief moan did escape her, though, and for an instant, her father's gaze left Jared and flickered over to her.

In that split second, Jared moved. Afterwards, she was never able to understand how he covered that distance in such a remarkably short time. One hard chop to the wrist made her father grunt in pain, and drop the gun. Jared kicked it well out of the way. Then he caught hold of the lapels on her father's jacket.

'Now,' he said breathlessly, 'do we have to fight

over your daughter, like a couple of animals? Or are you going to sit down and talk, like a civilised human being?'

Her father didn't say anything at all, though. Instead, he just seemed to collapse, like a deflated balloon. Without the gun, all his bluster and menace seemed to simply dissolve away. His eyes weren't wild any longer, but became rather frighteningly blank and glazed. He half collapsed into a nearby chair, and then just sat there, staring at the floor with unnerving emptiness.

'What's the matter with him?' whispered Cassandra. 'Has he had some kind of attack? Oh, God, we'd better get a doctor!'

'No,' said Jared, with some certainty. 'It's not a physical illness. I think he's had some sort of mental blackout. He does need medical help, though. Psychiatric help,' he added with a brief frown. 'He's gone right over the edge, Cassandra.'

'I have to get him back to London,' she muttered. 'There'll be doctors there who can help him.'

At that, Jared lifted his head. 'You don't even need to get involved in this. I'll make the arrangements, get him to a place where he can be cared for and given treatment.'

She stared at him incredulously. 'What do you mean, I don't need to get involved? He's my father!'

'And he's done his best to damned well ruin your life,' Jared reminded her roughly. 'Let him get to you now, and he'll have succeeded.'

'Look at him!' Cassandra flung her hand out at the bowed, motionless man sitting in the armchair, apparently hearing and seeing nothing of what was going on around her. 'Do you really think he's any kind of threat any more?'

'Yes,' said Jared implacably. 'When he was healthy, you stood a good chance of getting away from him. Tie yourself to him again now, while he's like this, and there's every chance you'll end up a prisoner for the rest of your life.'

'I don't believe I'm hearing this,' she said in disbelief. 'You've got to be the coldest, most unfeeling man on this earth!'

Jared caught hold of her arm. 'Was that the way I seemed to you earlier?' he demanded harshly.

'I don't remember,' she said, with deliberate cruelty. 'All I can think about right now is my father.' She stared down at him. 'I did this to him,' she mumbled in mounting horror. 'All of it—*all* of it—was my fault.'

Jared gave her an unexpectedly violent shake. 'He did it to himself! If he'd let you grow up normally, let go of you like every parent should and allowed you to become an adult in your own right, it would never have come to this.'

Cassandra wasn't even listening to him any more. More and more, she was beginning to be consumed by guilt. She had run out on her father when he needed her, selfishly pursued her own life and independence, without giving a thought as to how it was affecting him.

Jared seemed to realise he wasn't getting through to her. Abruptly, he let go of her and backed off a couple of paces.

'What do you intend to do?'

'Get him into hospital,' she said, almost thinking out loud. 'You're right, he needs expert help.'

'And stay with him?'

'Of course,' she answered, without hesitation.

'For how long?'

'For as long as he needs me.'

'And what if that turns out to be for the rest of his life?' Jared questioned her fiercely.

'I'll deal with that, if and when it happens,' Cassandra replied steadily.

'And where does that leave me?'

She looked at him almost in surprise. 'What do you mean?'

'What if I need you, too?'

For just an instant, his question startled her. Then she shook her head firmly. 'You don't. You're the most self-sufficient man I know.'

'There are different kinds of needing.'

'You want someone to share your bed?' she said bluntly. 'You're a very attractive man. You won't have any problems finding someone.'

'That wasn't what I meant,' Jared growled. 'And you damned well know it!'

'All I know right now is that I've got to give my father all the help I can,' she said in a voice that was curiously flat, but very clear. 'I can't run out on him, not while he's like this.'

'So, everything we have—it just has to be thrown away? All your independence that you talked about and wanted so much—that's got to be tossed out of the window, too?'

'Jared, stop it,' she said tiredly. 'You're confusing me.'

'Good,' he said grimly. 'Because I want to confuse you. Perhaps that's the only way of stopping you from going through with this. Cassandra, think what you're doing!'

'I know what I'm doing,' she retorted. 'I'm facing up to my responsibilities.'

'You haven't even thought about it.'

'I don't need to. It's a simple question of what's right and what's wrong. I'm sorry, Jared, I know it's not very fair to you——'

'Fair?' he cut in incredulously. 'Cassandra, don't you understand what I'm trying to say to you? You're not going to do yourself or your father any good by doing this. Why can't you see that?'

'All I can see is that you want me to put you first,' she threw back at him. 'And you're angry because I won't do that. You said you need me—and perhaps you really do, although God knows, you've never shown it. But from now on, my father needs me more. He doesn't have anyone else.'

'And I do?'

She didn't want to answer that question. Instead, she began gathering her clothes together. 'I'll get dressed and packed. Can you arrange some sort of transport? I don't know if we can get an ambulance all the way to London, but I'd be grateful if you could try. I don't think there's any other way to get him there.'

Yet still Jared didn't move. It was as if he couldn't quite believe she would really go.

'You realise you're suffering from shock?' he said evenly. 'If you'd only give yourself some time to think, you'd start to behave more rationally.'

'I can see things perfectly clearly. It's a question of priorities——'

His silver eyes suddenly blazed. 'And obviously, I come pretty low on the list!'

Cassandra stared straight back at him. 'What you or I want doesn't count right now. Things have changed. Why can't you see that?' Part of her couldn't quite believe she was saying all these things, not to Jared. Then her gaze swung back to the bowed, defeated figure of her father, and guilt washed over her again in great waves. It was because of her he was like this, a mental wreck. 'Are you going to phone for that ambulance, or do I have to do it myself?' she said in a flat, cold voice.

'I'll do it,' Jared growled. He went to turn away, but at the last moment swung back to her and gripped her wrist painfully hard. 'Change your mind,' he got out roughly, and there was almost a note of pleading in his voice. 'Cassandra, don't do this. Try and see sense!'

She tried to pull away from him, but couldn't. Suddenly terrified that she might weaken, that she might look into those silver eyes and see a whole lot of things that she couldn't bear to look at right now, she stubbornly refused to meet his gaze.

'You're just like my father,' she flung at him accusingly. 'You won't let me go!'

Jared's face went completely white with shock. An instant later, he released his grip on her, his fingers flexing and unflexing, as if they suddenly hurt.

'Oh, I'll let go of you,' he told her grimly. 'If you really think I'm anything like your father, then I've obviously not been getting through to you on any level. I happen to think you're wrong, but you're not interested in seeing things from my point of view. And while things are like this, I don't think there's much future for the two of us.' His silver eyes scanned her intently, but she still wouldn't look at him. 'All right,' he said flatly. 'You've made your choice—now you'd better live with it! I'll phone for the ambulance, and the two of you can leave.'

With that, he strode out of the room, leaving her with the silent figure of her father, and her own sudden hot and painful tears.

CHAPTER NINE

THE FIRST couple of weeks back in London seemed like a continuous bad dream. Getting her father into a hospital, the long talks with the doctors, telling them a lot of things that she would have much preferred to have kept private, yet couldn't because they needed to have so many background details before they could begin to treat him. Then, almost too tired and drained to think, the effort of trying to pick up her old life, to get her interior design business going again, even though she had absolutely no interest in it any more. And, all the time, the memories of Jared in the background, intruding relentlessly on her days—and her nights—no matter how hard she tried to keep them out.

Things improved just a fraction once she finally managed to establish some sort of routine. Work in the mornings, taking on only small commissions so she could take off a couple of hours every afternoon to visit her father. She dreaded the visits, yet forced herself to go through with them. To cover her own feelings, she talked to him brightly about the past, about the times they had shared together back in her childhood. Her father had come out of the almost catatonic-like state he had been in when they had first brought him in, but he wasn't the same man he had been before. The bluster, the confidence, the ruthlessness had all gone, but there didn't seem anything there to take its place except a quiet apathy.

The only thing that seemed to arouse a spark of interest in him were her visits. He seemed to live for them, as if they were the sole thing that kept him going.

And that kept the guilt in her alive and thriving, because there was one thing she had been forced to admit to herself very early on. She felt desperately sorry for him, and she hoped he would eventually get completely well again, but, try as she might, she just couldn't feel any love for him. She came out of a sense of duty, and pity. She knew it was wrong, that he was her sole surviving parent, and she *ought* to love him, but it was impossible. Sometimes, she thought that she had never loved him, and that made her feel even worse.

November came and went, and there were times she thought she would go a little crazy herself, but she didn't. Work helped to keep her sane. That, and the knowledge that she had to keep going, in order to keep up the endless round of visits to the hospital.

Then, on one visit, at the very beginning of December, the doctor who had been treating her father came out just as she was leaving.

'Do you mind if I have a word with you before you go, Miss Gregory?'

'Of course not.' She followed him along the corridor, to his small office.

'Come in and sit down,' he invited.

'Is something wrong?' she asked anxiously. 'Is my father worse?'

'No, he isn't.' But before she could sigh with relief, he added, 'But neither is he getting any better. I think you must have noticed that yourself.'

'I thought he seemed a little more cheerful today,' she said slightly defensively.

'I don't think there's been any noticeable improvement,' the doctor said crisply. 'That's why I'd like to ask you if you'd agree to a fairly radical change in your visiting arrangements.'

Cassandra's heart instantly sank. 'You want me to come more often?' she said, hoping he couldn't hear the dread in her voice. 'Mornings, as well as afternoons?'

'Quite the contrary,' replied the doctor. 'We'd like you to cut down your visits considerably. In fact, we'd prefer it if you came just once a week, and stayed for no more than half an hour.'

Cassandra simply gaped at him. 'But—why?'

He sat back in his chair, and didn't reply at once. Finally, though, he tapped his pencil thoughtfully on the table and said, 'When your father was first admitted, you told us quite a lot about your home life, and your relationship with your father. You were very frank, and we appreciated that. We've also had a chance to talk to your father at length, and I have to say that my overall impression is that this close relationship you have is very much one-sided. He can't seem to live without it—but you deeply resent it, and want to break away, so you can get on with your own life.'

Cassandra was about to hotly deny it, but at the last moment she remained silent and slumped back in her chair.

'There's no need to feel in the least guilty about it,' the doctor went on more gently. 'Yours is a very healthy attitude to take, Miss Gregory. It's your father's attitude we have to try and change. And to be honest, I think we have a much better chance of achieving that if you aren't around.'

'But you've just said he can't live without me!'

'That was the wrong choice of word,' said the doctor. 'I should have said "won't", not "can't". He's quite capable of living his own life. It's just that, for reasons of his own, he's chosen not to. That isn't fair to himself. And it most certainly isn't fair to you.'

'You mean that I'm actually doing him harm by staying around?' she said incredulously.

'If you want to put it bluntly—yes,' said the doctor. 'If you're always there, he'll simply lean on you more and more, until he ends up being totally dependent. That'll be a disaster for him, and a nightmare for you.'

Cassandra suddenly felt very cold. Although he had used different words, Jared had said virtually the same thing. Yet she had refused to listen to him, had broken up their relationship because she wouldn't believe him.

The doctor was looking at her sympathetically. 'I'm sorry if this has all come as rather a shock.'

Cassandra gradually began to recover her wits. 'To be absolutely honest,' she said slowly, 'it's a relief.' She looked up at him. 'Does that sound awful? But I hated those visits so much.' She shuddered. 'Some days I had to force myself to walk through the door. I know how that sounds, but I can't help the way I feel. I don't *love* my father,' she blurted out.

'There's nothing at all unusual about the way you feel,' the doctor assured her. He gave her a brief smile. 'And you're not a monster. There's nothing unnatural about not being able to love a parent. Sometimes, it works the other way round. Parents find they can't love one—or even more—of their children. And brothers and sisters are notorious for falling out, perhaps going for the whole of their lives without speaking to each other, or having any contact. Family relationships are really no different from any others. Sometimes they work out, and sometimes they don't. Only, we feel much more guilty if we can't love a member of our family because we've been brought up to believe it's very wrong, almost a sin.'

'You're right, I do feel guilty,' Cassandra admitted in a low voice. Then she lifted her head and looked directly at the doctor. 'Will my father really get better more quickly if I'm not around?'

'I'm certain of it,' he replied. 'It'll take time, of course—we're probably talking about months, not weeks—but he's basically got a strong character. And once we can make him accept that he's got to build an independent life for himself, that it isn't fair of him to demand to share yours to the point where there's no room for any other relationships for either of you, I think you'll see a radical improvement.'

Cassandra shook her head slowly. 'You're going to find it very hard.'

Unexpectedly, the doctor smiled. 'Don't worry. I think we're up to it. Just leave it all to us.'

She still couldn't quite believe that the crushing burden had been lifted from her shoulders so completely.

'You're sure I can't help?'

'Absolutely certain,' the doctor said firmly. He paused for a moment, then added, 'You do know why your father couldn't let go of you, don't you?'

'Not really. He's always been very possessive. When I was young, I thought he was just being over-protective, and it would get better as I got older. It didn't, though. In fact, it got worse.'

'There's a good reason for that,' the doctor said gently. 'It's because you look so much like your mother.'

Cassandra's head shot up. 'My mother? I don't understand,' she said, in some bewilderment.

'From the talks I've had with your father, it's very obvious he never got over your mother's death. He couldn't get interested in relationships with other women, so gradually his personal life became entirely centred around you. And the older you got, the more you grew to look like your mother. In his mind, you started to take her place. It was almost like having her back again.'

Cassandra gave a brief shiver. 'That's rather sick, isn't it?'

'It's certainly not healthy,' the doctor agreed. 'Although it wasn't perverted in any way. His feelings for you weren't sexual. In every other way, though, he began to confuse you and your mother in his mind. It was why he was so extremely possessive, why he tried to keep you close to him all the time. And why he finally cracked when he found you with another man. He couldn't stand the thought of you loving someone else, and belonging to them instead of him. It was almost like having his wife run off with a lover.'

'Perhaps it's my fault,' she muttered. 'I should have stood up to him more, left home earlier, got right away before things reached this stage.'

'Don't blame yourself,' the doctor said immediately. 'None of this was your fault. And don't feel guilty about leaving him to face this on his own. Believe me, it's the only way he'll make any sort of recovery.' He looked at her squarely. 'Do you want my advice, Miss Gregory? It would be to get out of here, and get on with your own life.'

Yet it wasn't quite as easy as that. She walked

away from the hospital knowing that she ought to feel free, but the next few days seemed oddly empty. Without the regular visits to the hospital, the afternoons seemed to stretch on for ever, and, no matter how hard she tried to work, she could never keep her mind fully occupied with what she was doing. One thought haunted her. She had turned her back on Jared so she could be with, and help, her father. But that help wasn't needed—had never been needed. Having her around was only worsening his condition.

So, what did she do now? She didn't know. One thing she was pretty sure of, though. Jared wouldn't want her back. 'Get on with your own life,' the doctor had told her. Yet she didn't know how to do that. She felt as if she were drifting in a sort of no man's land, with no aims, no ambitions, not even any really good reason for getting up in the morning.

To make it worse, it was getting near to Christmas. The shops were full of cheerful decorations and the counters piled high with tempting goods. She bought a few gifts for friends, and a dressing-gown for her father, but she was always glad to escape back to the quiet emptiness of her flat. She found other people hard to take at the moment. Friends had got in touch when they had heard she was back in London, but she had refused all their invitations and rarely left the flat except to go to work.

December dragged on, and seemed to turn into the longest month of her life. She made no plans for Christmas—in fact, apart from buying those few gifts, she simply ignored it. She worked until late on Christmas Eve, ostensibly picking out fabric samples, but in reality putting off the moment when she would finally have to go home.

At last, though, she pushed the pile of fabrics to one side and gave a brief sigh. She supposed she would have to leave. She couldn't stay here all night.

She was just about to switch off the light when she heard footsteps in the outer office. Instantly, she tensed. This late at night—and on Christmas Eve—the building should be virtually empty. Whoever was outside almost certainly had no business being there. And she was trapped in this inner office—a very convenient victim.

Then the door to her office opened, and Jared Sinclair walked in.

The sense of shock at seeing him was so great that she backed behind her desk, and then fell weakly into her chair.

Jared gently lifted one eyebrow. 'Now I know what they mean by the phrase "to bowl a maiden over".'

'I just didn't expect—I never thought—when I heard someone——' She tried hard to stop gabbling, and finally succeeded. 'I didn't think it would be you,' she finished, rather feebly.

'Were you expecting someone else?' The words might have been casual, but his tone definitely wasn't.

'No, of course not.'

Her reply seemed to please him, because he lounged in a more relaxed fashion against the doorway. 'I remember the first time I came here,' he remarked. 'Do you know what a shock it was when I first set eyes on you? I didn't expect Randolph Gregory's daughter to be a raving beauty, with a mass of gorgeous pale blonde hair and huge violet eyes.'

'You didn't look as if you were particularly impressed at the time,' she retorted.

'I wouldn't *let* myself be impressed. After all, I had come here with the firm intention of abducting you,' he reminded her.

Cassandra decided she didn't want to remember where all that had led to.

'What are you doing here?' she muttered.

'It's Christmas Eve.'

'I know that!'

'I don't think anyone should be on their own at Christmas, do you?'

She shrugged. 'That depends if you're feeling in a sociable mood or not. But if you're that desperate for company, I'd have thought there were plenty of places you could go.'

Jared's silver eyes briefly flickered. 'I was talking about you,' he said gently. 'You're the one who shouldn't be on her own.'

His attitude unaccountably annoyed her. She wasn't some lame duck who couldn't get through the holiday period on her own!

'So what is this?' she retorted. 'A charitable gesture? A "take someone into your home for Christmas" scheme?'

'You do like to make things difficult for yourself, don't you?' remarked Jared.

She stared at him in disbelief. 'How can you say that? You're the one who said I had to live with the choice I'd made. And since that choice didn't include you, I assumed I wouldn't be seeing you again.'

'I said a lot of things that afternoon that I deeply regretted later on,' Jared said in an unperturbed tone. 'And I'm ready to admit that my attitude was pretty selfish, expecting you to completely abandon your father in favour of me. My only excuse is that it's rather hard to be rational after a man's just pointed a gun at you, with apparently every intention of killing you. And it makes it even harder when the girl you love declares her intention of walking out on you, and going off with that same man.'

Cassandra blinked. 'The girl you love?' she echoed in a rather odd voice. 'What exactly do you mean by that?'

'I'd have thought it was fairly self-explanatory.'

'But you've never said it before. Not all the time we were at Glenveil. Not even on that day when I left.'

Jared still looked entirely comfortable. 'It takes me rather a long time to get round to some things. I thought you knew that.'

'I'm not sure that I know anything about you at all,' she said slowly.

'Then perhaps it's time you started to learn.'

She didn't know what to say to that. Instead, she just stared at him warily, still not at all sure that any of this was really happening.

'How's your father?' asked Jared.

The rather abrupt change of subject surprised her. 'Do you really care?' she challenged him.

'It's rather difficult to feel too much concern for someone who wanted to shoot me,' he admitted. 'But for your sake I'm willing to give it a try.'

'If you feel like that about it, don't bother!'

His gaze sharpened noticeably. 'Cassandra, why are you behaving like this?'

'Oh, no reason at all!' she retorted with heavy sarcasm. 'I mean, I know I'm being *completely* unreasonable. After all, we've only been apart a couple of months. And I'm sure you've got a dozen perfectly good reasons why you didn't write, or even ring. I just can't understand why I'm not flinging myself straight into your arms, absolutely delighted to see you!'

He didn't seem too worried about her outburst. A few seconds later, she found out why.

'Only someone who'd missed me like hell would get so upset,' he said, with some satisfaction.

'Oh, you are so conceited!' she said furiously.

Jared merely grinned. 'No, not conceited. Just fairly confident about certain things.' He paused, and his dark features became more sober. 'Are you going to tell me about your father?'

'There's been a very slight improvement,' she said at last. 'It's early days yet, but the doctor's hopeful that it'll continue.'

'You don't go and see him very often any more.' It wasn't a question, but a statement.

Cassandra lifted her head. 'How did you know that?'

'I've made it my business to keep track of things over the past couple of months.'

'You've been spying on me?'

'Just keeping a friendly eye on the situation.'

'Why?' she demanded.

Jared's silver eyes narrowed a fraction. 'I thought I'd already made that perfectly clear.' He levered himself away from the doorway, and came a little further into the room. Cassandra had forgotten just how imposing he could appear at times, and she huddled down a little further in her chair.

'I suppose you want to know why I stayed away for so long?' he went on.

'I'm sure you've got a very plausible explanation,' Cassandra said stiffly.

'I don't know if you'll consider it plausible, but it seems to make a lot of sense to me.' He perched on the edge of the desk, no more than a couple of feet away from her, and she tried hard not to look at him because it seemed to do funny things to her nervous system. 'After you'd left Glenveil, I couldn't see any point in coming straight after you, because you'd made your position perfectly clear. You were going to look after your father, and you just weren't interested in anything—or anyone—else.'

'I didn't say I wasn't interested,' she interrupted in a low voice.

'All right,' Jared agreed. 'Perhaps that was the wrong word. Let's just say that your conscience wouldn't let you stay with me. You felt a whole load of guilt over what had happened, and the only way you could try to get rid of that guilt was by ''doing your duty'', and being the loving, supportive daughter your father wanted you to be. Is that about it?'

'It's a very simplified way of looking at it. But, yes, it's about right,' she admitted.

'I thought if I gave you time, you'd eventually realise you were on the wrong track,' Jared continued. 'That you'd see your father would only get worse if you were constantly hanging around. It would just feed and strengthen his obsession for you.'

Cassandra twisted her fingers together edgily. 'The doctor told me more or less the same thing. I only wanted to help, to put things right,' she muttered defensively. 'Was that wrong?'

'Not wrong,' he said in an unexpectedly gentle voice. 'Just rather misguided.'

She sighed. 'I've made such a total mess of things.'

'You did what seemed the right thing at the time. It's all anyone can ever do. And I didn't help things by staying away too long. I should have come back before this.'

'Why didn't you?' she asked in a subdued tone.

'I suppose I needed some more time myself. I wanted to be sure of what I was offering you. Before I could be absolutely certain, though, I had to get my own life together again.' He gave a rather crooked smile. 'You want to know what I've been doing these last few weeks? I've been working.' He reached into his pocket and pulled out a small, brightly coloured box. 'This is only a prototype, but it'll give you a good idea what the finished product will look like.'

The first thing she saw was the name of the company, splashed across the corner of the box. Cassandra Toys.

'I know I only meant it as a joke when I first suggested it,' Jared said, slightly apologetically. 'But it seemed as good a name as any. Do you mind?'

'No. No, of course not,' she said a little dazedly. She lifted the lid of the box, and then stared at the small pieces of metal and plastic neatly packaged inside.

'When you fit them all together, it becomes a spaceship, doesn't it?' she said slowly. 'The spaceship you showed me up in your workshop, at Glenveil.'

Jared nodded. 'There are half a dozen different models—transporters, shuttlecraft, interplanetary ships. And I've finished the space station, as well. Kids will either be able to buy the models individually, or they can gradually collect them all and make them up into a much bigger playkit. And I'm working on an alien spacefleet, as well, so kids can play at repelling invaders from outer space. If everything goes well, I should be able to get them into the shops by next autumn. With some imaginative advertising, we should capture quite a chunk of the Christmas trade.'

'I'm glad you've got your life together again.'

'No, not quite together,' he told her, his face becoming very still. 'One large and very important part is still missing.'

But she was growing a little wary again now. It wasn't that simple. In fact, it wasn't simple at all.

'I couldn't ever seem to get through to you before,' she reminded him. 'You kept me locked out nearly all the time. Why should things be different now?'

'Because being away from you for so long made me realise one thing very clearly. I don't like being separated from you. As for not getting through to me—you damned well did!' he said in a suddenly husky voice. 'It's just that I'd never admit it.'

'But I can't simply pretend things are all right,' she said stubbornly. 'They're not.'

In one swift movement, Jared swung himself round to her side of the desk, grasped her wrists and pulled her to her feet, and then stared at her with eyes that were suddenly very bright.

'We can argue about this all night,' he muttered. 'But I'm getting tired of all these words. Let's try settling things in a more traditional way.'

He didn't give her time to protest. Another quick tug on her wrists brought her up close against him. Then his mouth was hungrily exploring hers, as if they had been apart for two years instead of two months.

Cassandra fought against him half-heartedly, knowing there was a lot more she had to say to him, but at the same time unable to resist the hard, comforting warmth of him, the delicious pressure of his lips and the sweet invasion of his tongue.

'Mmm,' he murmured in satisfaction, a couple of minutes later. 'It's even better than I remembered. I must have been insane to have stayed away for so long. I should have come down and just carried you off.'

'The way you did the first time?' she reminded him a little tartly.

'At the time, I thought that was the most irrational thing I'd ever done in my entire life. Looking back, though, I think it was definitely the most sensible.' He pulled her a little closer, and this time she didn't resist. 'You've stopped fighting me,' he observed, with obvious pleasure. 'Good. I like my women willing.'

'How many of them have you got?' she queried with mock indignation.

He didn't even bother to answer. Instead, he bent his head to hers again, and as he subjected her to another of those long, druggingly pleasurable kisses, his hands began to move over her restlessly, impatient to reacquaint themselves with the tantalising curves of her body.

Cassandra closed her eyes, her head dizzy with the irresistible mixture of love and pleasure. For just a few moments, she forgot that she had meant to be far more cautious than this, that there was so much that still had to be resolved.

Then Jared's hands suddenly stopped moving, and she felt him become oddly tense. Her own head began to clear, and she remembered—too late!—that she hadn't meant to let him this near to her. At least, not yet.

She tried to pull back, but he wouldn't entirely release her. One hand still gripped her wrist, while the other ran lightly over her breasts, down to her waist and hips, and then back to her breasts again.

Anyone watching might have thought it a lover's caress. Cassandra knew better, though. He can't know, she tried to reassure herself a little frantically. He can't!

His silver eyes came up to meet hers, and wouldn't release her gaze again.

'You're pregnant,' he said flatly.

Although part of her had been expecting it, his words still came as a shock. She hadn't even got used to the idea herself yet.

'I don't know for certain,' she muttered defensively. 'I was going to get a test after Christmas. It might be just a false alarm,' she added, with a touch of defiance.

Jared's expression didn't change. 'You don't need a test.' He held up his hand and she gazed, a little hypnotised, at his long, strong fingers. 'I can pick up two pieces of wood,' he told her evenly, 'and just by touching them, I know if one of them is a fraction thicker than the other.' Then he let his hand return to her body again. 'You've lost weight, you're thinner,' he went on. 'I can feel the outline of your ribs. But your breasts——' his fingers drifted against their underswell '—they're fuller. Not by much—not yet—but the difference is there. And there's a very slight swell to your stomach. I know you, Cassandra,' he went on in an unexpectedly thick voice. 'I can remember what every inch of your body felt like when I touched it. Don't tell me that I'm imagining the difference I can feel in it now!'

'You're so clever,' she flung back at him a little resentfully. 'It's a wonder you don't hire yourself out as a pregnancy testing service. You'd make a fortune!'

He ignored her response. 'Were you going to tell me?' he demanded directly.

'Yes—I suppose so.'

'When?'

'I don't know!' She glared at him angrily. 'I didn't know you were going to come marching back into my life again. I hadn't made any definite plans, I didn't *know* what I was going to do.'

And that, at least, was the truth. From the day when she had first suspected her pregnancy, she had pushed it right to the back of her mind and refused to think about it. It was one more complication in her life, and she had felt she just couldn't cope with it.

'Do you want the baby?'

Her eyes suddenly blazed. 'Of course!' Then she was immediately surprised at her answer. It was the first time she had admitted it, even to herself.

'Then you'd better take me along with it,' Jared told her. His face looked rather white, but his voice was quite firm.

'What do you mean by that?'

'It's a rather clumsy proposal of marriage.'

Cassandra's mouth set in a stubborn line. 'That isn't necessary. I'll manage.'

'My God,' he said in pure irritation, 'there are times when you drive me nearly crazy! I'd probably shake you, if it weren't for your condition.'

'I just don't think it would be a good idea,' she persisted, trying to keep her own voice steady, and wishing that her knees weren't trembling quite so much.

'Would you like to give me one valid reason why not?'

'You got married the first time just to give your child a name and a home. And now you're going to do the same thing all over again! Self-sacrifice isn't a good basis for a marriage.'

Jared shook his head in disbelief. 'And what exactly do you think I'd be giving up?'

'Well—your freedom, your independence.'

'Did I say I wanted either of those things?'

She gave an uncertain shrug. 'I suppose not.'

Jared sighed, and this time he did shake her, only very gently. 'Cassandra, haven't you been listening to a single thing I've been saying to you this evening? I came back because I love you and I want you. The fact that you're pregnant doesn't make the slightest bit of difference—except that I happen to be delighted about it. At least, I will be once I've got over the shock!' When she still looked unconvinced, he slid his hand into his pocket. 'I brought you a Christmas present,' he said more softly. The ring he slid on to her finger had an exquisite amethyst surrounded by small, sparkling diamonds. 'I chose the amethyst to match your eyes,' he told her. 'You can change it, if you want to.'

Dazedly, she shook her head. 'It's perfect,' she whispered.

'It's to remind you that you're mine,' Jared said huskily. 'At least, until I can get a gold band to go with it, and make the whole thing completely legal.'

'I don't know what to say——' she muttered shakily.

'That certainly makes a change!' Jared teased gently. 'But if you can't manage anything else, how about a simple "yes"?'

She couldn't even get that out, though. Instead, she just nodded happily, her eyes suddenly very bright.

'So—where would you like to spend Christmas?'

he asked her. 'It can be anywhere you like—as long as it's with me.'

She lifted her head and looked at him, her gaze still sparkling. 'I'd like to go back to Glenveil.' Then she almost laughed out loud at the surprise that clearly showed on his face.

'It'll be cold and draughty,' he warned her.

She slid her arms comfortably around his neck. 'We can stay in bed, to keep warm.'

'There'll be no hot water when we get there.'

'Then we'll make do with a quick wash. I *definitely* don't want you taking any cold showers,' she told him solemnly.

Jared grinned back at her. 'Don't worry. It would take more than a cold shower to have any effect on the way I feel whenever you come near me.' He glanced at his watch. 'If we leave now, we can drive overnight and be there by tomorrow morning. How does that sound?'

'Fine.' She sighed contentedly. 'It'll be very romantic, don't you think? Christmas in that big house, with crackling log fires and snow on the hills.' She looked at him a little anxiously. 'There will be snow, won't there?'

'Of course,' he said. 'I promise it.'

She suddenly looked a little wistful. 'I didn't get you a Christmas present.'

Jared laid his hand against her stomach. 'Yes, you did. Although it wasn't quite the one I was expecting!'

'Have you got over the shock yet?'

'Just about. Do I still look pale?'

Cassandra studied his face. 'No. In fact, you look a little bit flushed.'

'Mmm,' he murmured. 'Well, I told you what

happens every time you get close to me!' He bent his head and took one quick, fierce kiss; then he reluctantly let go of her again. 'We'd better stop right there, or I'll be in no fit state to drive!'

'You don't mind spending Christmas at Glenveil?'

'I don't mind spending it on the moon, as long as you're right there with me.'

'It's funny,' she said, 'but I really hated that house at first. Now, I can hardly wait to get back there.'

'It'll certainly be a very handy retreat whenever we want to spend some uninterrupted time together. Which will probably be quite often,' he told her huskily. He slid his hand through hers. 'Let's get going.'

And, for once, Cassandra didn't argue with him. In fact, she was quite certain that she was going to spend the next few days doing exactly what he wanted!

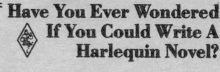

Have You Ever Wondered If You Could Write A Harlequin Novel?

Here's great news—Harlequin is offering a series of cassette tapes to help you do just that. Written by Harlequin editors, these tapes give practical advice on how to make your characters—and your story— come alive. There's a tape for each contemporary romance series Harlequin publishes.

Mail order only

All sales final

TO: *Harlequin Reader Service*
Audiocassette Tape Offer
P.O. Box 1396
Buffalo, NY   14269-1396

I enclose a check/money order payable to HARLEQUIN READER SERVICE® for $9.70 ($8.95 plus 75¢ postage and handling) for EACH tape ordered for the total sum of $_____*
Please send:

☐ Romance and Presents   ☐ Intrigue
☐ American Romance   ☐ Temptation
☐ Superromance   ☐ All five tapes ($38.80 total)

Signature_____
                                                         (please print clearly)
Name:_____

Address:_____

State:_____ Zip:_____

*Iowa and New York residents add appropriate sales tax.

                                                                AUDIO-H

HARLEQUIN'S "BIG WIN"
SWEEPSTAKES RULES & REGULATIONS
NO PURCHASE NECESSARY TO ENTER OR RECEIVE A PRIZE

1. To enter and join the Harlequin Reader Service, scratch off the pink metallic strips on all your BIG WIN tickets #1-#6. This will reveal the values for each sweepstakes entry number, the number of free books you will receive and your free bonus gift as part of our Reader Service. If you do not wish to take advantage of our introduction to the Harlequin Reader Service but wish to enter the Sweepstakes only, scratch off the pink metallic strips on your BIG WIN tickets #1-#4 only. To enter, return your entire sheet of tickets intact. Incomplete and/or inaccurate entries are not eligible for that section or section(s) of prizes. Not responsible for mutilated or unreadable entries or inadvertent printing errors. Mechanically reproduced entries are null and void.

2. Either way your unique Sweepstakes numbers will be compared against the list of winning numbers generated at random by the computer. In the event that all prizes are not claimed, random drawings will be held from all entries received from all presentations to award all unclaimed prizes. All cash prizes are payable in U.S. funds. This is in addition to any free, surprise or mystery gifts that might be offered. The following prizes are awarded in this sweepstakes: *Grand Prize (1) $1,000,000; First Prize (1) $35,000; Second Prize (1) $10,000; Third Prize (3) $5,000; Fourth Prize (10) $1,000; Fifth Prize (25) $500; Sixth Prize (5000)$5.

    *This Sweepstakes contains a Grand Prize offering of a $1,000,000 annuity. Winner may elect to receive $25,000 a year for 40 years without interest totalling $1,000,000 or $350,000 in one cash payment. Entrants may cancel Reader Service at any time without cost or obligation to buy (see details in center insert card).

3. Extra Bonus Prize: This presentation offers two extra bonus prizes valued at $30,000 each to be awarded in a random drawing from all entries received.

4. Versions of this Sweepstakes with different graphics will be offered in other mailings or at retail outlets by Torstar Corp. and its affiliates. This promotion is being conducted under the supervision of Marden-Kane, Inc., an independent judging organization. By entering this Sweepstakes, each entrant accepts and agrees to be bound by these rules and the decisions of the judges, which shall be final and binding. Odds of winning in the random drawing are dependent upon the total number of entries received. Taxes, if any, are the sole responsibility of the winners. Prizes are non-transferable. All entries must be received by March 31, 1990. The drawing will take place on or about April 30, 1990 at the offices of Marden-Kane, Inc., Lake Success, NY.

5. This offer is open to residents of the U.S., the United Kingdom and Canada, 18 years or older except employees of Torstar Corp., its affiliates, subsidiaries, Marden-Kane, Inc. and all other agencies and persons connected with conducting this Sweepstakes. All Federal, State and local laws apply. Void wherever prohibited or restricted by law.

6. Winners will be notified by mail and may be required to execute an affidavit of eligibility and release that must be returned within 14 days after notification. Canadian winners will be required to answer a skill-testing question. Winners consent to the use of their name, photograph and/or likeness for advertising and publicity in conjunction with this and similar promotions without additional compensation.

7. For a list of our most current major prize winners, send a stamped, self-addressed envelope to: WINNERS LIST c/o MARDEN-KANE, INC., P.O. BOX 701, SAYREVILLE, NJ 08871.

If Sweepstakes entry form is missing, please print your name and address on a 3" × 5" piece of plain paper and send to:

In the U.S.

Harlequin's "BIG WIN" Sweepstakes
901 Fuhrmann Blvd.
Box 1867
Buffalo, NY 14269-1867

In Canada

Harlequin's "BIG WIN" Sweepstakes
P.O. Box 609
Fort Erie, Ontario
L2A 5X3

LTY-H119

Wonderful, luxurious gifts can be yours with proofs-of-purchase from any specially marked "Indulge A Little" Harlequin or Silhouette book with the Offer Certificate properly completed, plus a check or money order (do not send cash) to cover postage and handling payable to Harlequin/Silhouette "Indulge A Little, Give A Lot" Offer. We will send you the specified gift.

Mail-in-Offer

OFFER CERTIFICATE

Item	A. Collector's Doll	B. Soaps in a Basket	C. Potpourri Sachet	D. Scented Hangers
# of Proofs-of -Purchase	18	12	6	4
Postage & Handling	$3.25	$2.75	$2.25	$2.00
Check One				

Name _____

Address _____ Apt. # _____

City _____ State _____ Zip _____

ONE PROOF OF PURCHASE

To collect your free gift by mail you must include the necessary number of proofs-of-purchase plus postage and handling with offer certificate.

HP-2

Harlequin®/Silhouette®

Mail this certificate, designated number of proofs-of-purchase and check or money order for postage and handling to:

INDULGE A LITTLE
P.O. Box 9055
Buffalo, N.Y. 14269-9055